Bill,
Ben
Becky!

BLOOD ON KING'S MOUNTAIN

Charles E. Hayes

DEDICATION

United States Patriots; past , present and future.

Special attention is given to USAF retiree and Artist, Robert W. Wilson. Added is special thanks for the use of his art work on the cover and throughout the book.

Also Artists Richard Luce (**richardluce**.com) and Pamela White (**whitehistoricart**.com) for allowing their work to be used in this book.

10/24/15

Dear Charles:

Reference our TP conversation, above date, by this letter, I am giving you permission to use any of my art work covering the period *(SIC)* en compast by your book.

Providing, of course, you excuse the mis-spelled words etc. in this letter. My 95 year old mind is not well!

In fact, nothing is well in my physical being at this stage.

I trust the above is suitable.

Sincerely,

Bob Wilson

CONTENTS

ACKNOWLEDGMENTS

- Museum of Appalachia in Norris, Tennessee.

- Artists: Robert W. Wilson, Richard Luce and Pamela White

- The Efforts of John Dabney Shane and Lyman C. Draper

i

The Ballad of King's Mountain

Ferguson's Defeat

Come all you good People, I pray you draw near.

A tragical story you quickly shall hear

of Whigs and Tories, how they bred a great strife,

When they chased old Ferguson out of his life.

Brave Colonel Williams from Hillsboro came.

The south Carolinians flocked to him again,

Four hundred and fifty, a jolly brisk crew,

After old Ferguson we then did pursue.

We march'd to Cowpens – Brave Campbell was there,

And Shelby, and Cleveland, and Colonel Sevier,

Taking the lead of their bold mountaineers,

Brave Indian fighters, devoid of all fears.

Like eagles a hungry in search of their prey,

We chased the old fox the best part of the day,

At length on King's Mountain the old rogue we found,

And we like old heroes, his camp did surround.

The battle did last the best part of an hour,

The guns they did roar – the bullets did shower,

With an oath in our hearts to conquer the field,

We rushed to the Tories, resolv'd they should yield.

We laid old Ferguson dead on the ground,

Four hundred fifty dead Tories lay around,

Making a large escort, it not quite so wise,

To guard him to his chosen abode in the skies.

We shouted the Victory that we did obtain,

Our voices were heard seven miles on the plain,

Liberty shall stand – and the Tories shall fall,

Here's an end to my song, so God bless us all.

                                        Author unknown.

Prologue

There was a lot to be said for being "overmountain" from North Carolina. At least I think so. I thought so back in 1780 and I still think so today.

Some said that we were called overmountain because we were over the mountain and across the line King George had said in his 1763 proclamation that we weren't allowed to cross. I guess we fooled him. Settlers commenced moving into the Watauga, Nolichucky, and Holston river valleys in the late 1760s and early 1770s. Most came from Virginia through the great Valley and some came from North Carolina after the Regulators were defeated at the battle of Alamance. Some of the settlers claimed that the land had been given to the colony of Virginia by the Cherokee in the 1770 Treaty of Lochaber, but nearly all of us knew that wasn't true ---- still, it was a good excuse. Of course, we were ordered to leave but we didn't leave.

Instead of leaving, we cut a deal with the Cherokee to lease the land for ten years in 1772. Not that any of us had any plans to leave but both we and the Cherokee pretended that we did. When the deal was cut, we established what we called the Watauga Association to establish the rules that we would live under. Later, in 1775, the Cherokee sold us the land outright.

This didn't put us in the clear by any means. In April 1775, the British in Massachusetts marched out of Boston to capture John

Hancock and Sam Adams and steal powder and guns while they were at it. They wound up being run back to Boston and the revolution was started. While there was a lot of distance between us and Boston, the war kept getting closer. To top it off, the British tried to get the Cherokee to go to war against us and some renegade Cherokee under Dragging Canoe, called Chickamauga, were more than willing to do just that. The main Cherokee Chiefs were more inclined to just let us and the British fight it out between ourselves.

That is not to say that all was peaceful between us and the Cherokee. The Cherokee were talked into whipping up an all-out fight against the settlements in July 1776. It didn't do the Cherokee or the British any good as we beat them like a drum. In 1777, the Cherokee signed the Treaty of Long Island, giving the American colonies the Watauga and Nolichucky valleys.

When the war commenced, we organized ourselves into the "Washington District," and pledged loyalty to all the united colonies. We formed a Committee of Safety that replaced the Watauga Association. We then petitioned North Carolina to be annexed to give us another source of military protection. The politicians in North Carolina, knowing a good thing when they saw it, annexed us in 1777. Since we were too far away to be taxed, we didn't really care what North Carolina said or did.

For some reason, we seemed to worry politicians and governments. In 1774, the Virginia governor, Lord Dunmore, called the Watauga Association a "dangerous example of Americans forming a government distinct from and independent of his majesty's authority." And here we just thought we were trying to put as much distance between ourselves and pettifogging governments as we could.

That's not to say we didn't do our part to help the Continental army and North Carolina. We just wanted to start our lives where things weren't already so messed up with rules and taxes so bad that a man had trouble getting his breath.

I reckon the first white men to settle in the Watauga Country were Julius Dugger and Andrew Greer. Will Bean and his wife Lydia started the first settlement in 1769 on Boones Creek. Their son, Russell Bean, is reckoned to be the first white child born in the region.

I reckon that men from our region fought in most of the Battles of the revolution. The rest of us hunted and farmed while we were on the lookout for Dragging Canoe and his Chickamauga.

1

NEWS

One of the things we always waited for, were eager for and received infrequently, was news. Just about any kind of news was welcome. If a letter was received, it was a natural fact that folks made their way to the receiver to find out what the letter had to say. The same with newspapers.

There weren't many newspapers but when one was available, everyone wanted to know what news was printed on the paper. We noticed that sometimes the letters we received didn't agree about how something happened and like as not, they didn't entirely agree with the newspapers. Sometimes, the differences made it a bit confusing but we still wanted to hear all the news we could.

Sometimes we got news we liked --- like when our army whipped Burgoyne in New York. It was good to hear that Burgoyne with all his lobster backs and Hessians could be whipped. Some folks took this to mean that General Gates was a fine general but some letters said that Gates didn't have a lot to do with the victory.

Some more good news came in the summer of 1778 when we learned that Washington and his Continental army held its own at the battle of Monmouth Courthouse. We got a letter that said Washington stopped a retreat ordered by General Charles Lee and cussed Lee up one side and down the other. After running Lee off the battlefield, Washington stopped the retreat and organized his army to fight.

The army fought. They stood against the British and did not even think about running. That was some good news that we held on to real close.

Lately, we weren't getting a lot of good news.

We learned that the British army under General Charles Cornwallis, with the help of the British navy, forced the surrender of Charleston. American General Benjamin Lincoln tried to negotiate an honorable surrender but was forced to surrender his force of over 5,500 soldiers under dishonorable terms.

The British continued to show their dishonor at the Waxhaws. Colonel Abraham Buford had been leading a force of around 400 Virginia Continentals towards Charleston but after a skirmish at Lenud's Ferry, he headed back towards North Carolina. General Cornwallis sent Banastre Tarleton and his Legion after Buford.

Tarleton moved his men and equipment quickly. With 300 men, Legion mounted infantry, Legion cavalry and regular British dragoons, Tarleton chased Buford at top speed. It is said that Tarleton moved his force a hundred miles in less than three days.

Tarleton caught up with Buford and sent an officer to demand surrender. Rather than surrender or stand and fight, Buford decided to try to retreat. When Tarleton's legion caught them, Buford started to place his men in a defensive line but it was too late.

Tarleton ordered his legion to charge. Buford's men waited too late to fire and the British ran over Buford's men like they were a coach road. Some of Buford's men ran and others tried to surrender. Unarmed with arms raised, they were murdered by Tarleton's Legion. Begging for quarter, they died.

So much for British honor and Tarleton's quarter. I didn't reckon I would ever trust Tarleton or the British.

Tarleton met up with Cornwallis near a place in South Carolina called Camden where they began operations. The British seemed to be in control.

Congress, being congress, decided the very solution to the problems in the Carolinas was to send a pet general to the Carolinas. Congress sent General Horatio Gates to rescue the southern states from the British. Some folks who knowed the Continental army weren't as high on Gates as the congress. We heard that his own soldiers called him "Granny Gates."

Gates seemed intent on proving his doubters right. He surely seemed to think that his reputation as the general who had defeated Burgoyne would take care of things in the Carolinas. Without taking steps to take care of getting his supplies or making sure his army was ready, Gates marched on Camden. We heard that he ordered his soldiers to be issued drinks of molasses and rum to keep their spirits up. It might have lifted their spirits but it also loosened their bowels.

Cornwallis arrived at Camden which over the next few months became an important base of operations for the British and in which supplies were assembled.

In July an American army under Major General Horatio Gates had marched from the north, arrived, and was threatening the British in South Carolina.

The British at Camden were led by Lord Rawdon, Cornwallis having returned to Charleston. Rawdon advanced from Camden to meet the Americans and took a position on a creek to the North-East of the town but fell back when he heard of Gates' approach.

Fortunately, for the British, Cornwallis returned and set his army in motion to meet Gates. He set his force in motion on a night march to confront Gates.

Gates, with a temerity he was not noted for, set his forces in motion at night to attack Rawdon's forces at dawn. He would have been better off if he had spent more time establishing his supplies and making sure all his force had some training and discipline.

Instead, Gates issued the men the rum and molasses drink and set off for his dawn attack. The two forces met, nearly collided, in the dark.

Goth Gates and Cornwallis were surprised by the encounter but Cornwallis held the high cards because all of his soldiers were trained and disciplined.

Gates, on the other hand, had some trained and disciplined Continentals. He also had inexperienced North Carolina and Virginia militia, most which hadn't faced a trained British army.

The area they fought in was between two swamps. This gave the two armies a narrow front and no opportunity to flank the other. Cornwallis set up his army in two brigades with two battalions of Fraser's 71st Highlanders providing a reserve.

Gates set up his army with the regiments of the Continental Army on the right under Gist, Baron de Kalb's 2nd Maryland and a Delaware regiment. In the center, he placed the inexperienced North Carolina militia and his right the largely inexperienced Virginia militia under Stevens. The reserve was the 1st Maryland under Smallwood.

Gates' entire center was made up of raw, inexperienced militia. I reckon that Gates is an idiot.

He ordered the left wing of militia to attack the British units. His left advanced only to be met by the entire British counter attack along the whole line. The untrained militia, without bayonets and without discipline ran off the field as quick as they could. Their fleeing allowed the British to turn the flank of the American right wing where the Continental units were putting up a good fight. When Tarleton's cavalry attacked the American right wing in the rear, the American units broke. Our troops fled, chased by Tarleton's cavalry for twenty miles or more.

Gates fled the field with the first fleeing militia. It was reported that he rode the sixty miles to Charlotte before stopping. No one would ever speak of gates as a fighting general again. Baron de Kalb, a German officer in the continental army, did a real good job of commanding his men and displayed both his bravery and competence before he was killed.

The Battle of Camden. Work shows the fatal wounding of Baron De Kalb. A public domain print.

More bad news came from the Kentucky settlements. A British led force of Shawnee attacked two Kentucky stations. Using cannon, they forced the surrender of Ruddle's Station. The British guaranteed the protection of the captured but the Shawnee began murdering captives almost immediately.

Putting all the information together, I reckoned that the British and their promises could not be trusted. I said as much to Sally Bean.

"Dan Bowman, do you really think we have anything to worry about from the British over here?"

"Maybe."

"Do you honestly think they will send an army over the mountains to pester us?"

I leaned back against the corner of a rail fence. "Maybe. They been knowed to do such as that."

"Maybe? Well maybe I should just ask Seth White what he thinks, after all, he is twenty years old."

What Sally said burned me up so bad that I didn't see that she was funning me, so I answered real quick. "What do you need to ask Seth for. I'm eighteen-year-old and know as much as Seth knows. You're only fifteen-year-old and you don't know near as much as I know."

"I'm sixteen, near seventeen-year-old, and I reckon I know about as much as you do."

"Maybe, maybe not."

"Maybe-maybe-maybe-maybe-maybe-maybe."

"Yep, maybe."

"Well my pa told my ma that he didn't think the British would come after us over here."

What she said slowed me down and brought me back to good sense. Maybe it wasn't necessary to bring bad news or the possibility of bad news to womenfolk before a man had to do it. I figured it might be time to keep my mouth shut.

"Well Dan Bowman, have you got anything to say besides maybe?"

"Maybe."

"Dan Bowman!"

"What I mean is, I want to know what you think about it."

Now I wasn't telling the whole truth. I just figured that anything I told her would be something she would question and argue about. Neither did I didn't want to tell her enough that was contrary to what her pa had told her and her ma or to scare her. I guessed that the best way to do that would be to let her talk.

"Dan Bowman, just when did you start caring about what I might have to say about anything?"

"Oh, I always have. I've just been shy about saying it. I've always knowed you are a real smart woman."

Sally reached out and touched my arm and looked up at my face. "Dan, do you really care what I got to say?"

I figured I had no choice but to keep it up. "Sally, you better believe that I do but if you keep pestering me about it or start poking fun at me, I reckon I might have second thoughts on it."

"Dan Bowman, you needn't worry, I won't ever poke fun at you again. I've just decided that you are one of the smartest men I know or have ever heard tell of . . . ever."

I didn't know what I had let myself in for. Sally commenced a talking about everything. She talked about how the Cherokee had her so scared back in 1776. She told me how scared she was of Dragging Canoe and his Chickamauga. I kept looking at her eyes and she kept on a talking. She talked about how beautiful the mountains are and how alone we were during rough winter weather. She talked about how fresh garden stuff was so delicious after a winter of meat and dried food. Then, just when I was sure she was about talked out, she surprised me.

"Dan, I've always wondered what it would be like to kiss you."

"What?"

"I've always wondered what it would be like to kiss you. Haven't you ever wanted to kiss me."

"I don't reckon I ever kissed a woman except my ma."

"So you reckon I am a woman and not just a girl."

I wasn't sure what I had got myself into but she wasn't arguing with me or pestering me so I nodded and said, "I reckon you are a woman."

As I said it, looking into her eyes, I wanted to kiss her. I leaned closer to her. As I leaned closer, her eyes closed and I kissed her cheek. Sally moved her head so that her lips touched mine and we both kissed. We kissed until we heard her sister, Abby, calling her.

We pulled apart, both of us breathing a bit hard. Sally spoke first, "I'd better answer her."

I just nodded. Kissing Sally was like nothing I had ever done.

"Over here Abby."

"Where?"

"By the fence."

"Okay."

Abby came running up like a Chickamauga was chasing her. "Pa wants everybody to meet at the church. There is news from the war."

Abby looked at me and added, "I reckon everybody will be there."

It didn't do any good to ask Abby questions because she only knew what her pa had told her. We caught up with my ma and pa before we got to the church.

"What's going on Pa?"

"We just been told that there is news of the war and that it will affect all of us."

"I reckon it will. Are they looking for men Pa?"

"I don't know yet but could be."

My ma turned on me like a dog about to grab meat. "Daniel don't you be getting any ideas about going off to no war. You're too young!"

Now I knew I wasn't too young but I knew better than to sass my ma. I had learned from my pa. He never argued with ma but he always got his way.

I slowed a step and squeezed Sally's hand. She squeezed right back. Right then I wasn't thinking about going to war. I was thinking about kissing Sally.

I didn't even know who was going to be speaking until Abby said, "Look, it's Seth."

2

War News

It was Seth. He looked tired. He was drinking water from a gourd and eating cornbread with a piece of meat. From the way he was attacking the food, I reckoned he had missed a few meals.

It being hot for September, Preacher Samuel Doaks had been telling the folks to go find some shade and sit outside the church. He kind of kept an eye on Seth while he greeted the families arriving and pointed out shady places where they could sit.

I was wondering about Seth's older brother Jack when I saw him sitting, leaning against a tree. Jack was taking his time with his meal of cornbread and meat. He seemed to be paying more attention to drinking water.

Just as soon as Seth finished the eating the meat and cornbread, drinking all the water from the gourd dipper and wiping his mouth on the sleeve of his shirt, Preacher Samuel Doaks stood and said, "Will everyone bow their heads and join me in prayer."

By Preacher Samuel Doaks' standards, it was a short prayer. It was thorough but it was quick for one of Preacher Doaks' prayers. After he amen'ed his prayer, Preacher told us, "I reckon you want to hear the news Jack and Seth brought us. Since Jack's still eating, we'll let Seth speak first."

Then Preacher Doaks patted Seth on the shoulder and stepped back.

Seth's Story

Ike Shelby knew, like all of us did, that our militia time was about up. Trouble with that was we still had a right smart of fight left in us and while we knew we needed to get back home and get things ready for the winter, we wanted to hit the British another good lick or two, hell, maybe three. Shelby talked to Colonel McDowell and the next thing we knowed, we were follerin him and Colonel Clark to attack a passel of Loyalists at Musgrove's Mill.

Others joined up with us. One of them was Colonel Jim Williams. His home was somewhere around Musgrove's Mill and the British and Loyalists had done run him off from his own home. He was real valuable to us because he knowed about every road, path and creek in the area. Val Sevier and a bunch of our Nolichucky men joined up too.

Now there was a rumor runnin around that the British army's war chest was at Musgrove's Mill with the Loyalists. It was a good rumor but I never saw no war chest.

Now Colonel Isaac Shelby was a fightin man and a knowin man. He knowed that our best chance was to travel quick and without being seen. Follerin Jim Williams, because he knowed the country best, we commenced to travel about an hour before sundown sometime in the middle of August. We moved through the woods until it got too dark, then we got on a road and follered it all night without stopping. We crossed a bunch of creeks whose names I don't remember and passed within two or three miles of Major Patrick Ferguson's camp. We were then within fifteen miles of Musgrove's Mill and had to step up our pace to get there by dawn.

As it was, it was near dawn when we got to within a mile of Musgrove's. Me'n four others who knew the country better'n I did went ahead to scout the territory. We forded Cedar Shoal Creek, just a piece below Musgrove's Mill and easy made our way about a mile above Musgrove's. Up there, we forded the Enoree River and Injuned up close to the Tory camp to spy them out. We took a good count and started to return the same way we had come. Right after we crossed cedar Shoal Creek, we run square into about ten or twelve Tories on patrol. They fired at us with their Brown Bess muskets and we returned fire with our rifles. I think we killed two and wounded three of the Tories. The rest turned and raced their horses back to the Tory camp just as quick as they could go. Two of us were wounded. We didn't waste time getting back to Ike Shelby and the rest to give our report.

The Tory leaders turned out to have more nerve than sense. They left a hundred men to guard their camp and the rest lit out to catch us. Shelby and Clark put us on a ridge with a lot of timber to use for cover. We were in sight of the creek. We weren't more than half a mile from Musgrove's Mill. While we were waiting, a farmer who lived near came to us and told Ike Shelby that the tory camp had been reinforced by two hundred men from the New Jersey Loyalist regiments and a hundred Tories on their way to join Ferguson.

Now that news put us in between two bad choices. It appeared that the force we faced was too large to attack and we, and our horses, were too tired to retreat. Shelby told us that we would fight.

We began to drag poles, old logs, fallen trees and brush to make a breastwork. While we did that, some of the men took our horses behind us out of the line of fire and tied them where they would be safe. When we had finished, the breastwork stretched in a half oval almost three hundred feet long.

Shelby and Clark didn't seem worried but they were busy. They placed about twenty mounted men on each flank so they could help any spot that needed help. A party of some two dozen men went to meet the enemy force. Their leader, Shad Inman, led them til only the river was between the two parties and fired at them. Before the Loyalists could fire, Shad ordered his men to retreat.

The plan was for the British force to chase the retreating men while Shad and his men made a big show of a fighting retreat. That is exactly what the British force did. The British saw our breastwork when they were less than two hundred yards away and commenced shooting uphill at the breastworks. Mostly, they shot too high.

We picked our targets, took aim and fired. We used trees and rocks for cover and a few used a fence as well as the breastwork. We had been told not to shoot until we could see the whites of the Tories' eyes;" or, as another has it, "till they could distinguish the buttons on their clothes. As if that weren't enough, we were told to hold our fire until told to shoot. I guess the colonels didn't want us to all have empty rifles at the same time.

They needn't have worried because the British had gone crazy. As soon as they saw Shad begin his retreat, they commenced to beat drums, blow bugles and holler Huzza for King George! They commenced shooting when they were just under two hundred yards away and kept charging and hollerin like a bunch of crazy Chickamauga. Of course, none of their muskets hurt any of us from such a far distance so maybe they were counting on sticking us with their bayonets.

We held our fire until they got to within, maybe, sixty yards. Then we opened up like a thunderstorm in the Smoky Mountains. That first volley caused them to flinch a right smart but they kept a coming and still outnumbered us. A large force hit our right wing and drove us back even though we killed a sight of them. They sure thought a right smart of their bayonets.

While we fought and were slowly driven back, Clark on our left held against Tories who didn't use the bayonet as good as those we faced. Clark, seeing that we had it pretty rough, sent his mounted reserve to lend us some help. It was a good thing too. It was still rough until Will Smith shot the main leader of the provincials. Will, he hollered out, "I killed their leader!"

Shelby took the confusion of the enemy to our advantage and had us charge them, all of us yelling like devils or Indians. Bayonets or no bayonets, we forced them back. We didn't just push them back. We killed another captain and wounded half a dozen provincial officers. Rob Bean himself shot and wounded Major Fraser. The Provincials were beginning to lose heart and the Tories attacking Clark were already looking for an excuse to run.

A British captain tried to rally the enemy but we killed him before he got good and started. When the captain fell, Clark and his men commenced a yelling and charging we were doing for Shelby. We were slashing with knives and tomahawks. The British and Tories lit out a runnin like they was late for dinner. They were a yelling and screaming so bad that they gave up on trying to fight back. They just threw away their muskets and ran to cross the river to get away from us.

The British retreat turned into a runaway. We chased after them and when we could, we killed them. We captured some though after they had surrendered. More should have surrendered. The ones who didn't surrender we tried to shoot. One man crossed the river and turned his hind end at us. Golding Tinsley shot him in his hind end.

Another Provencal who made it across the river tried to hid behind a tree. Trouble was, the tree wasn't big enough and Tom Gillespie shot him deadern a dry well.

We weren't through yet. We had rode all night and had just fought one hell of a fight but we weren't through yet. I heard that a man, a captain, named Sam Moore aimed to cross the river and raise some hell with the Tories so I followed him and ten or so others. We went up the river out of sight and crossed to the other side. Then we moved back toward the enemy and when we got close, we commenced a yelling and shooting them. We must a done a good job of it because they lit out a runnin and probably aint stopped ner slowed down yet.

Before we crossed back over the river to join Shelby and the rest, we met with two boys who didn't have any better sense than to hang around watching us fight. The said that the British reserve had run off before the Tories had retreated across the river. They said the reserve hollered "We are beaten — our men are retreating," grabbed their gear and lit out towards Ninety-Six faster'n a hen catching a June Bug.

It wasn't long before women and other folks from the area came to the baffle field. It wasn't a pretty sight to see the women checking the fallen Tory dead and finding that a husband, son, father or close friend had been killed. It was a sad sight and Shelby gathered us up to leave.

Shelby left a rear guard to watch for any enemy that might try to foller us. Sure enough, it wasn't long before a big patrol came riding toward the river just as hard as they could ride. Their shiny uniforms and flashing swords and scabbards fairly sparkled in the early morning sun. They stopped to talk to someone at Musgrove's Mill, then rode like the dickens to cross the river. The rear guard claimed that the sun hit the water splashes in such a way that made them look like rainbows.

The rear guard watched from the tree line until they were across, then rode to rejoin Shelby. Of course, the British were too late to do anything except help the wounded and bury the dead.

We later heard that for the rest of the day, from miles around, Tory women and children continued to come to the battle field to see if a loved one had been killed. I guess that's the very nature of war.

Shelby had just got us moving after the enemy which was moving toward Ninety-Six when a rider from Colonel McDowell caught up with us. His news changed everything. He told us that Gates had been totally whipped at Camden and most of the army killed, wounded or captured. He said that Gates got away and was likely still running.

Shelby and his officers talked it over and decided the best thing to do, for the time being, would be to avoid the chance of a run in with Ferguson and get with McDowell. And that is just what we done.

General Gates might a plowed a deep furrow up north but he dern sure didn't show it in the Carolinas. I know sure as sin that Ike Shelby could a done a better job.

Shelby and his officers spread the word that, for the time being, we would avoid the chance of a run in with Ferguson and join with McDowell. It made sense to all of us.

We didn't have a lot of choice about going back to McDowell. We had a passel of prisoners to watch over and we had Major Ferguson to avoid. It's not easy to fight and guard prisoners at the same time. Instead of returning the way we had come, which would have meant moving in a north east direction, we went to the northwest over rougher country.

Like Shelby figured, it wasn't long before Ferguson was a chasing after us. Neither men nor our horses had been able to rest but I figured that I could take as much hard times as Ike Shelby could. Anyhow, there wasn't time to rest while danger follered us so close. We did stop a few times to rest our houses and let them and the men get a bite to eat. Some of us pulled roasting ears of corn off the stalks and ate them without having time to cook them. We found some good peaches too. Both men and horses were able to drink from the many creeks we crossed.

We were lucky. On our second day of march, our rear guard told us that Ferguson arrived at one of our stopping places no more than half an hour after we left. They spent two hours feeding their horses and resting, then they turned back. Our rear guard follered them for the rest of the day until they camped for the night. Then the rear guard set off to catch up with Shelby. They didn't catch up with us until we were almost at the end of our march because Shelby didn't stop. We traveled through the night and didn't stop until late the next day when we reached the camp.

We had traveled over sixty miles, with over seventy prisoners, through the hottest August I can remember. It was constant travel for almost fifty hours. I don't reckon I have ever been so worn out as I was then.

I took care of my horse and took a nap ... a long nap. While I slept in the shade, McDowell, Shelby and I guess some other officers talked it over and decided to raise an army of volunteers from both east and west of the mountains. Of course I don't know exactly what was said but that was the grist of it.

They had Colonel Williams and Captain Hammond take the prisoners to Hillsboro. The governors of North and South Carolina were both there and I reckon that Williams laid it on thick that he was the leader of the expedition and he was promoted to Brigadier General of the South Carolina Militia. It's a sight what lies some men will tell for a little glory.

I wouldn't trade one Ike Shelby for ten like Williams.

Jack's story

Well, I'm surprised that Seth didn't tell you how he whipped half the British army by himself. I got to say my little brother has been known to windy a mite --- especially when pretty girls are around.

From what we were told, Cornwallis ordered Ferguson to move into Tyron County with his militia. Privately he said that he had little or no respect for the Loyalist militia. Ferguson did as ordered and followed the Patriot militias into the back country of North Carolina. Ferguson unleashed bands of his militia to search for Patriot leaders. These Tory militia raided mostly at night, plundering and looting where they rode. They forced Patriots to take loyalty oaths to the king or die.

Patriot leaders learned not to sleep at home at night. Neither did they tell their family where they would be hiding so the Tory militia could not get the information from them.

Patriot families began to gather at the largest best defensive house in the region with their arms, ammunition and valuables. Less than ten miles north of King's Mountain, Colonel Will Graham's home was such a place. It was a big, hewn-log-house, and fortified. It was ready for a defense against any militia armed with muskets or rifles and no cannon.   In early September, I was there when a band of two dozen marauding Tories rode up to Graham's.

The Tories demanded to enter. Will Graham refused and the Tories attacked. They stood and fired several volleys that didn't do any real damage, didn't even get through the window shutters. The Tories cussed us and ordered that we surrender.

One Tory ran up to the house, and through a port hole, fired at a man named Will Twitty. Susan Twitty saw the musket in the port hole pointed at her brother and pulled him out of the way. Susan ran to the hole and looked out to see the Tory reloading his musket. She grabbed Will and hauled him to the port hole and told him, "Kill that son of a bitch!"

Will fired, hitting the Tory in the head, killing him deader than Job's turkey. Susan wasn't through yet. She opened and ran out the door, grabbed the Tory's musket and ammunition and returned with them to the house. After seeing the Tory killed and with several wounded, the Tory band retreated.

Colonel Graham suggested we move to a safer place a few miles away, which we did. A large band of Tories then attacked the empty house and stole everything they could take away, including six of colonel Graham's slaves.

Now is a bad time for Patriots in North and South Carolina. After Gates was shipped and Sumter's force scattered everywhere between hell and breakfast, the Tories were riding high. Patriots had to either run, fort up or sign loyalty oaths pledging loyalty to King George the Turd.

Some of the Tories, some of them would rather be called Loyalists, are pulling in their horns a bit. They are the ones paying attention to partisan fighters like Francis Marion who the British call

"The Swamp Fox," and other leaders and wonder if maybe the British could lose.

Too many Tories think the war is already over and that they lost. Some of these are the ones who are persecuting Patriots and stealing everything and every slave they can. They figure that when the dust settles they will be the rulers and everybody else will be their subjects.

These are the Tories that are murdering, raping and stealing.

These are the Tories that are willing and ready to bring this same cruelty over the mountains to us.

Adam Reep returned home after his militia duty ended. He had no sooner got home when a dozen Tories led by a British officer rode up. Reep saw them in time to bar his door and get into his loft with rifle and a musket he had took off a dead British soldier. Reep fired through port holes, killing one and wounding two before they retreated.

But a lot of our people are discouraged. When Ferguson was headquartered at Gilbert Town, he sent word out for folks to come to him to take an oath of allegiance to the crown. Folks figured that since Charles Town had been taken, Gates had been whipped, Sumter surprised and his men scattered and no other patriot forces to be seen, that they had no choice but to sign the oath. They were less afraid of the British army than they were of the Tory militias.

The men who signed these oaths of allegiance did so not because they wished to surrender but to protect their wives, children and property. They felt they had no choice and most still aimed to fight against the British when they got the chance.

Ferguson didn't stop with getting oaths signed. He led a force to attack Colonel McDowell. He fought McDowell as he and his men were retreating toward the Watauga. McDowell learned where the British had camped and sent small bunches of men to strike them with quick hit and run attacks. He tried to damage the British and escape before they could close with him. He ambushed Ferguson at Bedford's Hill.

McDowell ambushed Ferguson as the British passed. They hit the British but were so outnumbered that the British forced McDowell back. Hit and run ambushes by Major Joe McDowell, Captain Tom Kennedy, and others busied Ferguson so that Colonel McDowell was able to escape and make his way to the Catawba Valley right now. They will soon be in Watauga.

Colonel McDowell aims to tell the leading men in the Catawba valley to go to Gilbert Town and sign the oath so they can save their families, property and stock. He'll tell them they don't have to mean what they sign.

Neighbors and friends, we aint out of the war just because we have a few hills between us and the British. Whether we take the fight to them or we wait for the British to come against us with Indians and cannon like they did those stations up in Kentucky. Neighbors and friends, they will come!

I'd rather take a bunch of men who are half horse and half wildcat, go after the bloody British, find them and then whip them!

Sally

Sally was as excited and taken by the speech as anyone listening. She almost didn't notice when Dan's ma touched her arm. She noticed when her arm was given a jerk. She was half following; half being led away from Dan by his mother. They stopped when they were far enough away to talk without Dan hearing their conversation.

Without preamble, Matildy Bowman told Sally, "I don't want Dan going off on this fight."

"Will he want to go?"

"It don't matter if he does. I don't aim for him to go and if you got any care for him, you won't want him to go either."

"How can I stop him?"

"You can't stop him. I'll stop him. I just need you to back me up. You need to understand that men don't know half as much as they think they do and they'll get into enough trouble without us sending them to it with our blessing."

"Then what can I do?"

"You can back me up. Anything I say, you go along with. Dan will make you a fine husband someday real soon but you need to get used to handling him now. Without a woman to keep them in line, a man is bound to make mistakes and bad decisions."

"I'm not sure what I can do to change his mind if he wants to go off to war."

"Yes you do. You can make things so nice for him here that he just don't want to leave. Men are not that hard to manage. Women been doing it for years, ever since Eve got tired of the Garden of Eden and pulled Adam out of it."

Sally was quiet. She truly didn't know what to say. She wasn't sure that she understood the bit about Eve being tired of the Garden of Eden and pulling Adam out of it.

"There's one more thing Sally, as you will learn, women can control what their sons do and who they wed. Your ma will tell you the same thing. Men have wild ideas and women have to settle them down and get them going straight on the right path. Do you understand?"

Sally wasn't sure but she nodded anyway.

"Then you need to support what I say to Dan. I know you don't understand it yet, but you will. You can ask your ma and now that you're old enough, she'll tell you. Do you hear what I'm telling you?"

"Yes, but ...."

There's no buts about it. You need to be on the same page I'm on when it comes to Dan. I'll help him see that it is you that he needs to wed and real soon. Do you see what I'm talking about?"

"Yes."

"I'm so glad, real glad, that you understand. There's one more thing, I wouldn't have Dan married to a woman who couldn't keep him going straight on the right path."

With that, Matildy walked away, over to where Sally's mother was sitting and began a conversation.

3

Threat News

Jack's speech had been interrupted several times with the crowd laughing at his humorous remarks about his brother. His speech was ended with cheers. While we were cheering, a horseman rode up to Jack. Jack waved and stepped back as the horseman handed Jack the reins of his horse and took his place. He stepped to the stump Jack had just left and waited for quiet.

Despite the dust from travel and his bearded face, we recognized him as John Sevier. When there was quiet he began without wasting time with nice talk.

"Does anyone here believe that distance and the mountains will protect us from the British army and their Tory lap dogs. The British have been trying to raise the Indians against us. The Chickamauga are already with them. What will happen when the red coats bring the Chickamauga and cannon against us just like they did last summer in Kentucky."

I could feel everyone around me sitting up to pay attention. I was leaning forward to make sure I didn't miss anything.

"The British will come after us because the British fear us. Cornwallis' problems did not come from General Gates and the Continental army. His problems came from Isaac Shelby and Shelby's overmountain men. We are not led by men like Granny Gates. We don't fight for parades. We are led by fighting men who fight to win! We fight for victories!"

Some cheers started but Sevier held out his hands to quiet the crowd.

"Our neighbors in North Carolina and South Carolina are being kept close to their families to protect them from raiding Tory bands. There are plenty of men who are ready to fight. They just need to know their families are safe and that they have leadership."

Preacher Samuel Doaks handed Sevier a gourd full of water. Sevier took the gourd and drank deeply before continuing.

"Ferguson fears us. Because he fears us he has threatened to cross the mountains and destroy us. He paroled Shelby's cousin, Sam Philips, with a message to us. Ferguson's message is that if we do not desist from our opposition to the British arms, he will march his army over the mountains, hang our leaders, and lay our country to waste with fire and sword."

Sevier had all of our attention.

"I say that fancy talking red coat won't have to come to us with his Indians and cannon. I say that we take the war to him and whip him like a borrowed plow nag. I say we beat him like a drum. We will beat him there before he can ever come over here."

Sevier took more water.

"Ferguson has Tories who know how to get here. Some are familiar with our region. One Tory was tarred and feathered by some of my light horsemen last summer to teach him a lesson. He didn't learn and has volunteered to lead Ferguson to our door steps. Before Ferguson can attack us, let's whip him."

Nothing could have stopped our cheers. Several men were standing and raising their rifles high.

"Isaac Shelby rode forty miles without stopping to make sure old Nolichucky Jack had the news about Ferguson's threat. We both agree that we should work together to defeat Ferguson!"

Sevier stopped, took a deep breath, and roared, "**Let's go get him!**"

That was when things began to get really wild. Men were shouting. A few fired their rifles up in the air, which I thought was foolish because now they would have to clean out the barrels. It was a waste of powder and lead.

Other folks didn't seem to mind. I heard men my age hollering that would go with Sevier and watched as they ran up to sign up. Pa got up and started to the stump where a quill and parchment had been brought. I got up aiming to do the same when two hands grabbed my shirt and jerked me back down hard.

"What do you think you are aiming to do Dan?"

I tried to turn but Ma held tight to my shirt. "Ma, I aim to go sign up so you let a loose of my shirt."

"I couldn't stop your pa but I can stop you. Both of you can't leave and your pa can take care of himself better than you can."

"Ma, you can't not let me do this."

"Yes I can and yes I will. Sally, don't think you should go either."

"I bet she does. You tell her Sally."

I looked at Sally and saw that she was staring at Ma, their eyes were met straight as a String.

"Tell her Sally."

Sally's eyes didn't leave my ma's eyes. "Dan, maybe you should listen to your ma.

"Hiram, come here," Ma called to Pa.

Pa glanced at her, took a drink from a jug that someone was passing around and walked back over to us as though it were his own idea.

"Is anything wrong, Matildy?"

"Your son Dan here seems to think he should leave me and Sally without protection and go off with you and Jack Sevier to fight the British. He don't seem to appreciate that the womenfolk left behind need to be protected too or the Chickamauga could just come and steal us away or worse."

Pa turned to me and lifted his right eyebrow. I had seen him do that before. It meant that there was no use arguing with ma and that we would have to go along with what she wanted.

"Dan, your ma is right. As long as I am going on this shindig with Sevier and Shelby, you will need to stay home and take care of the women. Now if I wasn't signed up to go, it would be a horse of another color, right Matildy?"

"Right, Hiram. There aint a bit of use in both of you a going against the British."

"There you have it Dan. I'm signed up to go and both of us can't go. I'll be the one going unless something happens to me, right Matildy?"

"Right!"

Ma stopped right there and looked at pa then at me. I could tell that she was going over everything that had been said and was examining it for any loopholes she might have missed.

"Right, Hiram. One of you will go and one of you will stay and you are signed up to go already."

Now I had been raised to respect my Pa and Ma but I sure didn't feel real good about the way the wind was a blowing now. Pa was looking at me and I saw him jerk his head a little toward Sally.

That sure slowed me down. I didn't aim to throw a fit like a little young'un in front of Sally.

I stood, reached for Sally's hand and asked, "Sally, if you're ready, I'd love to walk you home."

Sally glanced at the group that was beginning to celebrate then turned back to me. "Dan, I'd love to have you walk me home."

As we walked out of sight and hearing of the crowd, Sally pulled me to her and stopped. Looking at me with both hands holding me, she said, "I said I wanted you to walk me home. I didn't say I wanted to get there in a hurry."

Sally

Sally walked with Dan, holding his hand and thinking about what his ma had told her. She wondered if his ma could really keep them from marrying if they ever decided they should. Neither Dan nor she had ever mentioned marriage but she knew many women younger than she was who were married and expecting children.

"Dan, how long have we knowed each other?"

"Well, I was seven years old. I reckon you must a been just a baby."

"Dan, I was five years old."

"I guess you were."

"So it's been over ten years. We have knowed each other for over ten years. How come you never kissed me before today?"

"You were always poking fun at me before, you didn't today. I reckon that's why. I like kissing you though. I wisht you had stopped poking fun at me two or three years ago."

"I wish I had too. I like it when you listen to me. I don't think anybody ever listened to me like you did today."

I kissed her. I was getting used to kissing her in a big hurry.

"What do you think about what your ma said about you not going with John Sevier?"

"My pa always said I should always listen to my ma."

Sally wasn't sure his answer was to the question she had asked. Thinking about a few minutes, she was sure it wasn't. She stopped and pulled herself close to Dan and looked up at him. She responded to his kisses eagerly. When they were both out of breath and close to trembling, she stopped and gazed up at him.

"Dan, what if I asked you not to go with Sevier to war?"

"Sally, your voice is nicer than a bird singing. I'll always listen to you."

Once again, Sally wasn't sure her question had been answered.

Women and children had reason to fear British soldiers. Public Domain print.

"Dan, if you had to go, would you come back to me?"

"Yes."

"Then if you have to go, I'll wait for you."

"I would be counting on it."

4

Campaign News

I didn't have a lot to do with getting things organized. What I know I learned from watching and listening.

Everyone knew that Sevier, Shelby, Arthur and Will Campbell, Prescott and other leaders had a rare combination of leadership, bravery and commonsense. We reckoned that if a man had to go to war, that was the kind of leader to follow.

As I saw it, their aim was to raise all the men they could and whip Ferguson. It goes without saying that they would have to make sure the men had provisions and came with the right weapons and gear. This force of men would then try to surprise Ferguson either in his camp unawares or on the march unawares. If they weren't able to do that, they would gather all the help they could find and take the fight to all the redcoats and tory groups they could find.

They intended to win but if the British put too many men against them for them to win, they would undertake a fighting retreat to their families and travel by water further away from the British --- all the way to Spanish Louisiana if they had to go that far.

We were told that Colonel Charles McDowell and Colonel Andrew Hampton with about one hundred and sixty men, had retreated from Ferguson's army and joined with Colonel Carter and his men. They were now camped on the Watauga.

Sevier and Shelby talked with McDowell and his officers to gain their knowledge of Ferguson. Sevier continued to look for anyone who could give him news about Ferguson and Shelby made contact with patriot forces in Virginia. He wished to gain the support of Colonel Will Campbell and his fighting men. Everyone agreed to meet at the Sycamore Shoals of the Watauga River on September 25th.

I reckon that Shelby was busier than a man fighting hornets. While trying to reach other leaders, he still had to make sure his own regiment was ready to march and fight. Now he didn't try to do everything himself. He had his brother, Moses, write to colonel Campbell letting him know what was planned and asking him and his men to help.

Shelby knew things had to be done in a hurry. He had heard from a farmer selling corn to the British that Cornwallis aimed to meet up with Ferguson and take the war into North Carolina. They also aimed to get the Chickamauga to attack the Holston and Watauga settlements. After the Chickamauga finished with the Holston and Watauga settlements, they were to go on to Chiswell's lead mines and kill the people there.

It seemed that destroying the lead mine operations was a big deal for the British and Colonel Campbell had been busy keeping Tories away from the lead mines.

Campbell let Shelby know that he aimed to raise as many men as he could and march through Flour Gap and meet Cornwallis if he came up from Charlotte instead of joining Shelby and Sevier's force. Shelby sent word to Sevier of Campbell's message and put out the call for all Sullivan County Militia.

Sevier's spies had told him that the Cherokee were going to attack the border settlements. Both Shelby and Sevier knew that enough men would have to be left behind to protect the settlements. Both knew that it would take big force to whip Ferguson and that it would take a big force to stay behind to protect the families. No man wanted to ride off to whip Ferguson and then return to find that his family had fallen to Chickamauga tomahawks and scalping knives.

Shelby sent a second message to Colonel Campbell. This time he gave his concerns more strongly. He let Campbell know that unless he joined with Shelby and Sevier, that they would not be able to leave behind enough men to protect the settlements and families left behind. Shelby strongly stated that if enough were left behind to protect the settlements and people, that there would not be enough to attack Ferguson.

Shelby also contacted colonel Arthur Campbell telling him of Ferguson's threats to the region and their intention of whipping Ferguson before he could attack the Holston and Watauga settlements. He let Campbell know that McDowell's force had been forced to leave their homes and seek refuge and asked for help in returning these brave men to their families.

Shelby figured that Art Campbell would want to help and he was both Will Campbell's cousin and brother-in-law. Shelby was right. Art Campbell had just talked with Virginia's governor, Thomas Jefferson, about turning the British tide that had been rising since Gates' defeat at Camden.

Arthur and William Campbell, after studying about it, agreed with Shelby and Sevier. They then sent word by a rider on a fast horse that they would be part of the campaign against Ferguson. Art Campbell sent word to Shelby that "The tale of McDowell's men, was a doleful one, and tended to excite the resentment of the people, who of late had become inured to danger by fighting the Indians, and who had an utter detestation of the tyranny of the British Government."

Both Colonel Campbell's got together with their militia officers and talked over their possibilities and plans. They decided to leave half the militia forces to protect their families and homes. The other half would join Shelby and Sevier in the campaign against Ferguson. Reports from the meeting said all the militia was as excited about the campaign as we on the Holston and Watauga were.

Riders were sent with messages telling the plans to Colonel Cleveland, of Wilkes County, North Carolina. He was asked to meet the campaign with his men on the east side of the mountains. I reckon the whole country was excited.

Sally tried her best to make me feel better. She said that if I was off on the campaign that we couldn't see each other or practice our kissing but, as much as I liked kissing Sally, I didn't want to miss the campaign.

Getting the campaign provisioned wasn't easy. Very few people had ready money and what they had wasn't much. Sevier tried to borrow money but there was none to lend. Sevier was reduced to going to John Adair, the State official for the sale of North Carolina lands and asking him for the loan of public money.

Adair answered him, "Colonel Sevier, I have no authority by law to make that disposition of this money; it belongs to the impoverished treasury of North Carolina, and I dare not appropriate a cent of it to any purpose; but, if the country is over-run by the British, our liberty is gone. Let the money go, too. Take it. If the enemy, by its use, is driven from the country, I can trust that country to justify and vindicate my conduct — so take it."

Due to John Adair's common sense, Sevier now had over twelve thousand dollars to pay for provisions his expedition. Both Sevier and Shelby pledged to repay the amount if it was not legalized by the legislature.

Everybody was excited except me. Ma was still bound and determined that I would be part of the force that stayed home to protect the settlement. She said both me and pa couldn't go and that pa was better able to take care of himself than her baby boy. So while the whole country was all heated up about going after

Ferguson and whipping him and his outfit, I was bad out of sorts.

Sally's efforts to make me feel better worked some. She said that she was afraid that I would find some other woman if I rode off with the army. I couldn't make her understand that as much as I loved a kissing her, I felt like I had a duty to go. I didn't want to have to say later that while my neighbors were a whipping the British, that I was too busy practicing kissing Sally to go with them. The truth is, I truly like to be kissing Sally. I just didn't want to miss out on the campaign.

I was trying to get used to the idea while I was trying to wear out an axe splitting a pile of firewood when pa called me. I turned and saw that he was on the ground trying to get up. I ran over to help him.

"What happened?"

"I was trying to throw the pack over the rail and did something to my back. Help me to the door so I can sit for a spell."

I helped him to the cabin door which had three steps leading up to it. He eased himself down and sat slowly.

"Bring me whiskey Dan?"

I went for the jug as we were seen by Ma.

"Hiram, what in the world happened to you?"

"Matildy, I was throwing the pack over a rail and did something to my back."

"Hiram, you need to lay down."

"Matildy, oh Matildy, I can't. I've got to finish packing for the campaign."

"Hiram Bowman, don't you talk foolish. You aint in no shape to go on no campaign. You're staying right here. I don't want to hear no arguing about it."

"Matildy, I believe you're right. I aint going nowhere any time soon."

"Of course I'm right. You're staying right here."

"Could you get me a stick to help me get up and move, Matildy?"

"Of course, of course."

Ma was getting him a walking stick when I got to him with the jug of whiskey.

"Dan, I reckon you heard your ma. She said I aint going nowhere. I reckon you better get packed and get over to the Sycamore Shoals before you get left behind."

"I'm on my way."

"Dan, go hug your ma first. Don't say nothing to her. Just hug her and go."

I ran over to where Ma was picking out a stick. Without speaking, I grabbed her and hugged her tight, kissed her on the cheek, let her go and lit out for the horse.

Ignoring Ma's voice behind me, I grabbed my rifle and gear. I turned to pa but he waved me off.

"Go Dan. Now!

I swung onto the saddle and went.

Isaac Shelby as he may have looked in 1780. (Taken from an original painting by Richard Luce (richardluce.com) used with artist's permission

John Sevier as he may have looked in 1780. (Taken from an original painting by Richard Luce (richardluce.com) used with artist's permission

5

Sycamore Shoals

I arrived at Sycamore shoals on the morning of September 25th. I was by no means by myself. Colonel McDowell and his men had been there for several days. It was undeniable that McDowell's men raring to get an even chance to fight the Tories who had once been their neighbors and fellow North Carolinians. I figured it was a sight how bad an enemy a former friend could be.

Things were busy when I got there and they got a sight busier. It also got a sight more crowded. What with Colonel Campbell's 200 men, Shelby's nearly 250 men and Sevier's' nearly 250 men added to what McDowell had, we were getting together a right smart of an army. Before the day was over, the other colonel Campbell, Art, arrived with two hundred men to give us a good crowd.

Everyone was busy, especially the leaders. McDowell left to encourage the people in North Carolina and get news of Ferguson's whereabouts. He also aimed to light a fire under Colonel Cleveland to get his men on the march.

I had to admit I had never seen so many men in one place before. Some were dressed in hunting frocks or wamuses made of linsey-woolsey or homespun. Some wore wool clothing and a few, like me, wore buckskin. Hats ranged from tricorns to flat brimmed hats and some made of otter, badger or coon.

I don't recollect seeing any muskets or fowlers in the crowd but there might have been some. All the men I saw were armed like me with long rifled barrel guns. We each carried a knife and tomahawk and a large wallet of food, mostly cornmeal. Most of us carried a tin cup and a few carried skillets.

A few beeves were brought along to provide rations but they slowed us down so much that we left them after the first day's travel. Everybody reckoned speed was more important than full stomachs.

We left the Sycamore Shoals the next day, on September 26th. Before we left the Rev. Samuel Doaks, prayed over us. He prayed a barnburner. He asked for the lord's Devine protection and guidance for us and threw in a few bible quotations to get us all in a fighting mood. He closed with the bible quotation, "The sword of the Lord and of Gideon." When Reverend Samuel Doaks said amen, we answered: "The sword of the Lord and of our Gideon's!"

A call to Arms at Sycamore Shoals. richardluce.com Art by Richard Luce and used with artist's permission.

With that, we mounted our horses and fell into line. We were in a big hurry to get to Ferguson but when we stopped at noon, we had only traveled a bit over three miles. Part of the reason for slow going was the slow beeves we had with us. Part of the reason was most of our horses were more used to pulling plows or wagons than being ridden. Some horses began to show the need for new shoes or having their shoes tightened. Some of the beeves stampeded and we had to take the time to gather them up. But we kept on until we had covered around twenty miles for the day and stopped to camp beside the Big Doe River. With plenty of fresh water for man and beast, we settled in and mended anything that had shown itself in need of mending. A man named Miller who lived nearby had a small forge. He real quick fired up his forge and shod a bunch of our horses that evening. I never did hear if he was paid or just did it to help us.

That night, we killed some of the beeves and cooked the meat. Our leaders had decided that the beeves were more trouble than they were worth. While we were sitting around fires and eating, I remembered what my pa had told me about being in places like this.

"Dan," my pa had told me, "I think a man is better off to listen much and talk less. Listen and use your common sense to know what is brag or idle talk and what is worth listening to from a man. Unless you have a big important thing to say, it is usually better to keep quiet."

So I wiped down my rifle, checked over my bridle and saddle and repacked my provisions. There was a lot of talk a going on. A lot of it was brag. Some of it made me think the speaker knew what he was a talking about. A man about my pa's age came over and sat beside me.

"Be you Hiram Bowman's boy?"

"I am."

"I see he worked things out with your ma so that you got to come along."

"Who are you mister?"

He offered his hand and I took it.

"Me and your pa are cousins. I'm with McDowell. I ran into

your pa a few days ago when he came to our camp near the Sycamore Shoals. He sure told me that your ma was dead set against you coming on this shindig. He told me that he got her to say that only one of the two of you could go - - - which he figures means that if he don't go that you could go. I reckon his back is a sight better now."

"Are you telling me that my pa didn't hurt his back?"

"Your pa was of two minds about whether he should go or whether he should maybe let you go into danger. I told him I'd be along to help you if you needed help."

"You got a name?"

"Dan, my name is Nathaniel Bowman. You can call me Nate. Everybody else does."

"Well Nate, I want you to be sure to call me if you need to be helped out of trouble."

Nate chuckled and told me, "I'll be sure to do that."

With that, Nate got up and walked toward where McDowell's men were camped. He was still chuckling.

6

Path to War

Our getting started the next morning went a sight easier than it had leaving Sycamore Shoals. Of course one reason was we had got the kinks out or out traveling. For another, we left the beeves we hadn't killed and butchered behind with Miller. I don't know if it was payment for all the blacksmith work he had spent most of the night doing for us or what. If it was, we got a fair trade.

Four hours after leaving the Big Doe River, we were traveling down the mountain on Bright's Trace which we followed through a gap between the Yellow Mountain and Roan Mountain to the south. It was a sight easier going down the mountain than it was coming up. The trace was only about as wide as a foot-path but it sure was easier going. Since it was still September, some of us were surprised to see snow on the tops and sides of some of the mountains. One of the men told me we were at the place called "The Bald Place."

The Bald Place was over a hundred acres of beautiful flat to rolling land. We stopped at a spring that ran through the land and drank deeply of the fresh, cold water. Those of us who had canteens emptied them and refilled them with this water.

It was at The Bald Place that the unexpected happened. Two of Sevier's men, Jim Crawford and Sam Chambers, deserted. Their absence wasn't noticed until later but we were sure they aimed to warn Ferguson.

To keep the suspected treachery from hurting us, our commanders changed our travel plans to use a more northward path in case Ferguson sent scouts to spy out the route we had planned to use. That night we camped at a spring that ran into Roaring Creek.

The Muster at Abingdon richardluce.com Art by Richard Luce and used with artist's permission.

The next day we finished traveling down the mountain. We reached land that *was still* green and in the warmth of Indian Summer. We tried to follow the path of less resistance but some of the path was dangerously rugged.

After a hard day's travel, we reached Cathey's mill and plantation. Sevier sent word to us that we had traveled over twenty miles since sun up. That night, we ate the rest of the butchered beef and parched corn from our wallets. It had been a rough day and we were tired so our rations tasted delicious. That night, I wondered what Sally was doing and if she was mad at me for leaving without saying good bye.

I was still wondering when I fell asleep.

Breakfast the next morning was the last of my journey cake from home and water. Our small army traveled up the valley of Grassy Creek, then through Gillespie's Gap. After we had passed through the Gap, we could see the upper Catawba in the distance. We divided to better spy the land for the enemy and information.

Campbell's men going south to Henry Gillespie's, and a little below to Colonel William Wofford's Fort in Turkey Cove. The rest traveled easterly on the old trace to the North Fork of the Catawba. Dividing the force seemed to make travel faster.

Colonel McDowell met Shelby and Sevier on the Catawba. He had sent Jim Blair to urge Cleveland and the men of Wilkes and Surry to hurry. Blair had been wounded but was able to meet Cleveland and give him the information.

While we rested, Nate Bowman came by to visit. He also brought some broiled pork which I gladly took.

"I appreciate the meat. Where did you get it?"

"It was a wild pig."

"Wild?"

"Could have been. The ears weren't notched."

"How are you and pa kin?"

"Our grandpaps were brothers."

"In North Carolina?"

"In Ireland. Our pa's came to the colonies as indentured servants. They wrote back to Ireland and when they got answers, the letter told where our pa's were at."

"Did pa really tell you to look after me?"

"He said to meet you and do what I could. All of us; me, your pa's, and you know that when the shooting starts there will be little we can do for each other."

"Pa knows I've been shot at."

"Your pa knows there's a sight of difference between being behind a wall and fighting off an Indian attack and meeting an enemy on a battlefield."

"I reckon I'll do alright."

"Your pa and I reckon you will too. We have no doubts about that at all."

"Your pa said you were smart. He said that you knew it did no good to argue with a woman and it was best to agree and then manage to do what you had to do."

I thought about that while I finished eating the meat Nate had brought. I was beginning to understand my pa a sight more. I could not remember him ever arguing with ma or raising his voice to her.

"This is good meat. Thanks."

"No problem. It's all part of kinfolks a looking after each other. You won't get so sore from riding horseback if you walk more at dusk."

With that, Nate got up and went back to his blanket roll.

We were told before we started the next morning McDowell had sent word that Ferguson was still in camp near Gilbert Town. We were also told that Cleveland and his men were making good time coming to join us and that other forces from South Carolina were on the way. What it boiled down to was that Ferguson was sitting fat and happy not knowing that we were in striking distance.

Two days later, Cleveland and his men joined us. Their meeting up with us made us a sight stronger but all this travel with provisions having to be hoarded was beginning to tire us. Worse than that, some of us were beginning to get careless. One of the Surry men, I don't remember his name if I ever heard it, was bad hurt when he fell off his horse. He was hurt so bad that he had to be left with a family of patriots to recover.

Worse yet, Colonel Cleveland's younger brother, and I can't recall his name either, was shot while crossing the Catawba river by a Tory. We later learned that the Tory thought he had killed colonel Cleveland instead of wounding his younger brother. The wounded man was left in the care of Colonel McDowell's mother who lived close by.

The next day was Sunday but it wasn't a day of rest. We traveled almost twenty miles that day. We did rest the next day a bit. For the first time since we started, we were rained on. I figured we were lucky to have had a week of good weather to travel in.

Rain wasn't the only reason we had to stop. Some of the men had begun to get restless enough to start rubbing each other the wrong way and there had been some push back against some of the rules the men had to live under. Shelby, Sevier and the other leaders talked it over and decided a leader of the whole force should be appointed. The sent a rider to General Gates to ask for a General to be appointed to lead the force. The idea was that the appointed general would hold a daily council to tend to any problems that came up.

Colonel Shelby pointed out that they might not have time for Gates, who he regarded as slow in everything except retreating, to act on the request.

The need to place a good man in command of the total force was agreed to by all of the officers. All the officers except Colonel Campbell were North Carolinians and Colonel McDowell was both commander of the district and the highest colonel we had.

Colonel Shelby had doubts that McDowell could handle the job and proposed Colonel Will Campbell take the leader position.

Campbell tried to talk Shelby out of this idea and told him that he should take the job. Shelby reminded Campbell that the was the youngest colonel and had served under McDowell. Shelby felt such a change in the positioning of him and McDowell would be bad for moral among McDowell's men. He told Campbell that as a Virginian, he would not be opposed by any of the different North Carolina leaders.

Shelby later explained pushing Campbell to be the forces leader by saying "I made the proposition, to silence the expectations of Colonel McDowell to command us — he being the commanding officer of the district we were then in, and had commanded the armies of militia assembled in that quarter all the summer before against the same enemy. He was a brave and patriotic man, but we considered him too far advanced in life, and too inactive for the command of such an enterprise as we were engaged in. I was sure he would not serve under a younger officer from his own State, and hoped that his feelings would, in some degree, be saved by the appointment of Colonel Campbell."

I still wasn't sure about what was going on so I waited until I saw Nate.

"Nate, what is going on with all our colonels and why is a man from Virginia in charge now?"

"Dan, an army can't work with a passel of men thinking they are in charge. Every man has to know who is in charge and who their orders come from. In an army that has been going on for a while, the man in charge don't have to be so active because he will have aides to do his running around for him. This army don't have time right now to build such a set up. That means we have to have a commander that do his job with very little help or no help."

"Okay." I didn't understand it all yet but it seemed the proper thing to say.

"On top of everything else, if a Colonel from North Carolina is put in charge, it might push him ahead of the other colonels from

North Carolina sometime later on. Putting a colonel from Virginia in charge won't change anything in North Carolina later on."

"I don't quite understand."

"Colonel McDowell is the highest Colonel from North Carolina we got. If a colonel with littler rank is put over him, he might feel his honor has been insulted and leave."

"So?"

"What if part or all his men leave with him. Remember, we are here to whip the British, not to argue over our own politics."

"I kinda understand but not really."

"That's close enough. Just remember, we are here to whip the British. That is the main thing we need to concern ourselves with, whipping the British."

"I got that part down pat, you can bet on that."

"Good, now did you draw your charge and tend to your rifle yet?"

"No, not yet."

"Then let's take care of our rifles."

We did.

7

Closing In

DIARY Entries of Lieutenant Anthony Allaire of Ferguson's Corps

Monday, 25th, and Tuesday, 26th. Lay at Gilbert Town; nothing extra.

Wednesday, 27th. Got in motion at five o'clock in the morning, and marched three miles to Rucker's Mill, and halted.

Thursday, 28th. Got in motion at five o'clock in the morning; marched seven miles to Mountain creek, forded it, although very difficult, continued on about a mile farther to Twitty's Ford of Broad river, and took up our ground on its banks. At six o'clock in the evening got in motion, forded the river; marched two miles to McDaniel's Ford of Green river; forded it, and marched two miles farther; halted on the road; lay on our arms till four o'clock the next morning.

Friday, 29th. We then, at that early hour, moved on three miles to one James Step's plantation, and halted. This man has been very unfortunate in his family; his wife, who is a very decent woman, was caught by the Indians about a twelvemonth past. They scalped and tomahawked her several times in the head, treated the infant she had in her arms in a most inhuman and savage manner. They mashed its head in such a manner that its recovery is truly astonishing; but what this poor, unhappy woman seems most to regret is the loss of her oldest son, whom the savages took, and she now remains in a state of uncertainty, not having heard from him since.

Saturday, 30th. Lay at James Step's with an expectation of intercepting Col. Clarke on his return to the mountains; but he was prudent enough to take another route.

Sunday, October 1st. Got in motion at five o'clock in the morning, and marched twelve miles to Denard's Ford of Broad river, and took up our old ground where we lay the 8th September.

Monday, 2d. Got in motion at four o'clock in the afternoon; forded Broad river; marched four miles; formed in line of action and lay on our arms. This night I had nothing but the canopy of heaven to cover me.

Tuesday, 3d. Got in motion at four o'clock in the morning;

marched six miles to Camp's Ford of Second Broad river, forded it and continued on six miles to one Armstrong's plantation, on the banks of Sandy Run. Halted to refresh; at four o'clock got in motion; forded Sandy Run; marched seven miles to Buffalo creek; forded it; marched a mile farther and halted near one Tate's plantation. John West came in camp, who is a hundred and one years of age; is amazingly strong in every sense.

Friday, 6th Got in motion at four o'clock in the morning, and marched sixteen miles to Little King's Mountain, where we took up our ground.

*　*　*

Despite what Nate had brought up about McDowell feeling that his honor was hurt and leaving, he seemed to take the decision like a gentleman. He did volunteer to take the message asking for a general to General Gates. He was thanked for his offer and it was pointed out that Colonel McDowell best knew the both the country and the temper of the people. The serious nature of his mission seemed to leave McDowell feeling better.

McDowell set off, leaving his command in the care of his brother, Major Joe McDowell. This seemed to set well with McDowell's men.

It was a good thing everybody was left in a good humor because we then passed through Burke county where McDowell's command was reinforced by kinfolks, friends and neighbors. If feelings had been different, we might have not got the reinforcements and could have lost men.

Colonel Campbell was recognized as the commander but all the colonels met every day to keep everything running right. The arrangement seemed to agree with the men as there was more talk of whipping Ferguson and less concern over who was running things.

Before we began our traveling on October 3rd, Colonel Sevier got all the men to form up in a wide circle. He told us that we were in for a good message that would interest us all. So we formed a large circle around Sevier and some of the other officers.

While we watched and waited, Colonel Cleveland got up on a fallen tree trunk and began to speak. "Men, I am here to tell you the news!"

It was something else to watch Cleveland get all wound up to let go a rip roaring harangue. He was a big, muscled man who weighed around two hundred pounds and could be as rough as a cob. But he did know how to get the men's attention.

"Now, my brave men, I have come to tell you the news. The enemy is at hand, and we must be up and at them. Now is the time for every man of you to do his country a priceless service. A service that shall lead your children to brag and exult in the fact that their fathers were the conquerors of Ferguson. When the pinch comes, I shall be with you. But if any of you shrink from sharing in the battle and the glory, you can now have the opportunity of backing out, and leaving; and you shall have a few minutes for considering the matter."

Well that might not have been exactly what he said but that is the best I can remember it and if it aint hundred percent right, it's anyway real close.

Anyway, it don't matter because the other officers took a run-a –go and jumped right into the mix. First Major Joe McDowell stepped up and hollered out, "Men, what kind of a story will you, who run away, will you who back out, have to tell your kinfolk and neighbors when you get home. Will you tell them that you left braver men to fight the battle, and win the victory?"

Then Ike Shelby stepped up, rared back and let us have it.

"Men you have been told. You have been given the offer and chance to run away, I mean leave. You have a few minutes to study it over. Then you will be given a chance to back out. When given the chance, if you want to back out, then step three steps to the back and stand.

Well, they waited a few minutes until Campbell ordered, "Ask the men."

This was followed by all the commanders saying real loud, "Any man who wants to back out, step three steps behind the line."

No man stepped back.

Shelby then roared out, I am glad to see that every man is resolved to whip your country's enemy. Let's go whip Ferguson.

The men cheered and I cheered with them.

Shelby lifted both arms until we were quiet and kept on speeching to us. "Men, when we meet the enemy, don't wait for orders. Each one of you be your own officer, and do the very best you can. Take every care you can. give yourselves of every advantage that you can. In the woods, shelter yourselves, and give them Indian play! Move from tree to tree. Press the enemy! Kill all you can. Your officers will not run from danger. We will be with you! Fight hard! Be alert! Obey orders!"

Me and every man there was ready to charge the gates of hell with a gourd full of water.

Shelby wasn't finished, he continued, "We move in three hours. Prepare two meals and pack them. Just before we mount up, we have some whiskey to pass around."

Now, Like I said, I can't swear I remembered every word right but I guarantee I got it real close.

The next day, we arrived at Gilbert Town. There, we were told that Ferguson had heard we were coming and had retreated. We were also told that Ferguson wanted to avoid fighting us.

We were also told that Ferguson had grown impatient about getting provisions and had become convinced that patriots were hiding their cattle. They forced Jack Carson to guide them to find cattle. He did so and showed the British a big herd of over two hundred beeves. The Tory's slaughtered over a hundred head of the beeves when one asked Carson who owned the beeves.

Carson made a big show of checking the ear markings and told them that he thought they might belong to Joe Brown, Dement, and Johnstone. This brought things to a quick stop because Joe Brown, Dement, and Johnstone were Tories in Ferguson's command.

We heard that none of the Tories in the region thought it was funny and a sight of them were bad tore up about it.

Of course, me, Nate and all the rest thought it was a right good tale.

We also found out that Ferguson had been warned that we were on the way and that we probably would not be able to attack him with surprise. A man named Robert Henry gave Shelby and Sevier the news. He was in such a hurry to tell it that some of us were around when he told them.

Robert Henry came running up to where Shelby and Sevier were looking at maps and hollered out, "Isaac!"

Shelby looked up and answered back, "Bob Henry, what's going on? Is the devil or some woman's husband after you?"

"Not yet. I came to tell you that Ferguson's been warned."

"How do you know this?"

"I was there when he commenced to calling for his officers. Seems two men who deserted from you had just come in and told him you're on the way to surprise him."

"Damn them! How did Ferguson take it?"

"Ferguson didn't take it as anything to laugh at, that's for sure. He told his officers that he had just heard that the 'back water men' were on the way and that they were mad about his threats of hangings, fire and sword and were coming mad and loaded for bear."

"How many men did Ferguson have?"

"Hard to say. He's just let a passel of them take some time off to visit their families and he had them sent for."

"Do you know what Ferguson was up to in gilbert Town."

"He and Cruger aimed to catch Colonel Clark between them. Clark has laid siege to Augusta, Georgia until Cruger came along from Ninety-Six to bust up his siege. When Cruger busted up the siege, Clark started making his way north along the east side of the mountains. Cruger sent messengers to Ferguson and they aimed to trap Clark between them and destroy him."

"Indeed."

"Yes, indeed. Cruger with his Tories and some Chickamauga were chasing so close that Some of Clark's men were killed. The Chickamauga scalped some of them."

"That's bad!"

"It gets worse. Captain Ashby and around twelve or fifteen captives were hung by the order of Augusta's Commander, Colonel Brown. Colonel Browne, who some say aint never had good sense, had been wounded twice during the siege. That made him maddern a wet hen. Brown gave around twelve to fifteen captives to the Chickamauga. The Chickamauga murdered them. Some were tomahawked. Some were tortured to death and some were burned at the stake. Over thirty men were murdered on Brown's orders."

"Is this Colonel Brown crazy?"

"Isaac, this Brown is crazy. He sent word to Ferguson that a bunch had been hung and a lot more would be hung. Brown's message to Ferguson said he had a, method for ending the war quick. Brown said they would hang every man that had signed an oath and was found to be against the king. Brown said the way was to catch them and hang them right then and there."

"It sure sounds like he is crazy."

"Ferguson said that was a good idea to hang all captives. He said that if they hadn't signed an oath, that they should have."

"We'll see what we can do about Ferguson."

"Ferguson's worried. When he heard from the two deserters of you coming to whip him, he did two things. He sent out messengers to get help and he started retreating toward safety. I reckon you scared the hell out of him."

"Good."

"The messengers he sent out carried a message that claimed you and your men aim to destroy him and for them to send him a lot of help real quick."

"How did you find out what the message said?"

"One messenger didn't get real far before he run square dab into a pistol ball. We took the message and everything else from him and hid his body in a handy hole."

"How handy was the hole?"

"Pretty handy. It must a took ten minutes to dig."

"Good work."

"We also got the letter that Ferguson sent with the messenger." Robert Henry handed a document to Shelby.

Shelby examined the document which read;

Gentlemen: Unless you wish to be eat up by an inundation of barbarians, who have begun by murdering an unarmed son before the aged father, and afterwards lopped off his arms, and who by their shocking cruelties and irregularities, give the best proof of their cowardice and want of discipline; I say, if you wish to be pinioned, robbed, and murdered, and see your wives and daughters, in four days, abused by the dregs of mankind-in short, if you wish or deserve to live and bear the name of men, grasp your arms in a moment and run to camp.

The backwater men have crossed the mountains; McDowell, Hampton, Shelby, and Cleveland are at their head, so that you know what you have to depend upon. If you choose to be degraded forever and ever by a set of mongrels, say so at once, and let your women turn their backs upon you, and look out for real men to protect them.

PAT FERGUSON,
Major, Seventy-first Regiment.

Later, when I got the chance, I talked the whole thing over with Nate.

We were resting, not saying much, so I asked him, "Nate, why do you think that the British and Tories are so ready to hang and kill us?"

Nate was quiet for a spell and I wondered if he had heard me and was just getting ready to ask again but Hate held up his hand, then answered my question.

"Dan, some folks will say that the way a person acts when they lose is how you know their character. That is partly right, not much but partly. Your pa told me once that you can judge a man's character not by how he acts when he loses but by the way he acts when he wins."

"My pa said that? I'm not sure I understand."

"Well, when a man loses, it don't do a lot of good to act up. It might not be his fault he lost but, unless he was cheated, he lost fair and square. If it is a fair and square loss, then hollering or crying about it only brings attention to the fact you lost."

"Okay, but what if you win?"

"If you win, even if you win by accident, it's harder to be humble and fair. It's easier to brag and want to rub the other man's face in his loss. I reckon that's what Brown done. He let winning give him the 'big head' and he wanted to rub the Patriot's faces in the dirt."

"I'd never - - - I hope I'd never do that."

"Sometimes it's hard not to do when you win. I reckon the best we can do is try."

"Do you think we have good leaders?"

"I do. Just look at how a bunch of them put their egos aside to choose a leader. Shelby came right out and said that as the youngest colonel, it shouldn't be him. McDowell swallowed his pride for the good of our cause and it seems that all our leaders are putting whipping Ferguson ahead of their personal feelings."

"I hope that if the time ever comes when I can either do what is best for me or do what is best for the country, that I do what is right."

"I hope so too, but it aint easy."

"Something else that aint easy is this marching or riding in a line and sitting at night. I'm getting restless."

"Dan, I'll see what I can do about that."

I took notice that the men didn't seem to be scared about the news of the killings and hangings. They all looked to making sure their rifles were ready and their tomahawks and knives were sharp.

There was another thing that struck me. From the way the men acted, I wouldn't want to be one of the two deserters who warned Ferguson. Not for a farm and a distillery, I wouldn't.

8

Treed

I was surprised when Nate came by early the next day. Too early because I was still asleep. He was leading his horse and mine. I noticed that he had a bit of a devilish look about him.

"I hope you're ready to ride Dan."

"Born ready and raised rough. What's going on and why this early? It's still dark."

"I volunteered to Major McDowell to scout and told him that you were the very man to go with me. When I told him about all your scouting experiences, he insisted you go with me."

"Experiences, what are you talking about?"

"Aint you been taught that it aint nice to point out that your kin might have stretched the truth a few miles or so? This gets you out of riding in line all day don't it?"

"Let's go!"

We went. We led our horses until we were outside the camping men so as not to disturb what little sleep they had left, then mounted. Nate led the way at a good pace. After a few miles he slowed up and we stopped.

It was just getting to light up a little bit and the air smelled fresher away from an army of men and horses. Nate dismounted and checked his saddle girth. I took time to do the same with my horse.

"Nate, what have you got in mind?"

"There's a farm about an hour from here where we can get fed and get information. We'll start there."

"I take it you know this country pretty good."

"Real good."

It didn't take quite an hour; it was just getting to be good light when we rode up to a good sized cabin. It was light enough to see that a big garden was part of the property. There was a barn but I didn't see any stock. The main cabin was separated from what appeared to be a cooking room by a covered dog-trot. I could smell coffee coming from the smaller cooking cabin.

Nate held up his right hand and slowed to a stop. I stopped beside him. I saw that Nate was looking around so I did too but I wasn't sure what I was looking for though.

"Where are the dogs?"

I got the idea that Nate wasn't asking me so I didn't answer. Then I saw a movement at the edge of the garden in some old cornstalks and whispered, "Nate, to my right, edge of the garden."

"I think you're right," he whispered. Gathering a deep breath he called out louder, "Hyar hound, hyar. Hyar David, hyar Goliath!"

"Pa!" A man who looked to be maybe fifteen or sixteen years old and a huge hound came running up. A woman came out the cook cabin holding a fowler and two boys who looked to be about twelve or so came from different directions.

Nate tossed me his reins and was out of his saddle faster than

I had ever seen him move. He met the woman halfway to the cabin and they grabbed each other. She was still holding her fowler and Nate still had his long rifle in his hand. I dismounted and handed the reins to the two youngest boys or young men. They looked to be somewhere between eleven and fourteen years old. I later found they were twelve and fourteen.

After Nate and his woman loosened their hold on each other, Nate motioned me over to them.

"Dan, this is my wife, Catherine. Those three wild ones are my sons; Hiram, Benjamin and Alexander. They mostly go by Ram, Ben and Sandy. My two daughters are still hiding."

"I'm pleased to meet you all."

"Cathy, this here is my cousin Hiram's son Dan. We have been chasing Ferguson. Right now, we're supposed to be scouting him. What do you all know to, make our job easier?"

Cathy began giving orders and shaping thing up in a way that Sevier and Shelby would have envied.

"Hiram, hide the horses and guard them. Give them as good a bait of feed as you can. Ben, run get your uncles and tell them I said they are already late. Sandy, run over to the Murphy's and tell them we need Jack now. Now move, all of you."

She sat us on a bench on the dog-trot and before I had time to do more'n stretch, she was bringing out hot food. There was coffee with cream and molasses, hot bread and butter, and cheese.

We ate quickly. The coffee was the best I'd had in a long time, maybe ever. Hot fresh bread with butter and cheese was such a treat that it tasted better than cake.

"That was delicious ma'am."

I was tempted but I didn't figure that unexpected company should take advantage and maybe not leave enough for everyone else. Part of me didn't want to, but I refused.

"Ma'am, I'm well filled. I feel spoiled as it is."

"If I'd known you were coming, I'd have had more food. I'd have had some meat. You know that don't you Nate?"

Nate savored the last of his coffee before he answered.

"I didn't know we were coming until I heard they needed scouts who knew the district. Then I talked Major McDowell into sending me and Dan. After I bragged us up so good, we need to take some pretty good stuff back with us."

"With everything that has happened around here lately, we can take care of that. It'll take nearly an hour for the boys to get the folks rounded up. Do you think you could use a nap?"

I had just started to say no when Nate jumped up and took his wife in his arms. He glanced at me and told me, "Dan go help Hiram with the horses and catch a nap while you help him look out."

I nodded, stood up, glanced around and saw Hiram motioning to me from the barn. I made my way quickly to him.

The barn was impressive. It was large, airy and clean. It appeared to have been freshly mucked out. I mentioned this to Hiram.

"We have to keep it clean. We keep the cattle away from the house and barn to make it harder for someone to find and steal them. Tories come by regular and always check the barn. If there is no fresh manure, they aint as apt to think we have stock that they can steal."

"Good thinking."

"A man will need a lot of good thinking if he's to survive this war. A lot of good thinking and he still may not make it."

I knew Hiram was right but there wasn't much I could add so I just nodded.

"There's some straw in the loft where you can rest. I'll wake you if anything happens.

I had already figured out that Nate had a large cabin that his patriot neighbors gathered at for protection. It sure was beginning to look like Nate was a leader to the people who knew him best.

I checked my horse and saw Hiram had already loosened the cinches and given them a good bait of feed and water. I figured they were apt to get worse spoiled than I was. I lay back on the straw and that was it until I woke from Hiram shaking me.

"Some folks are coming. Probably kin or friends but we can't be sure."

While Hiram tightened the cinches to the saddle girths and made the horses ready, I checked the priming of my rifle and made sure I was ready whichever way I had to jump.

When I saw Hiram's shoulders relax, I relaxed too. Moving up beside him I asked, "Is it kin or friends?"

"Both."

I saw Nate leave the house and walk over to the shade of a Huge Maple, four men joined Nate and twice that many moved to where they could watch for unwelcome visitors.

Taking both horses, having made sure the saddles and bridles were ready, I joined Nate and the others. I was glad to see that both Cornwallis and Ferguson had been well spied on by our people.

When we were all together, Nate pointed toward me and told the others, "I want you to know that this man is my kin. He's Hiram's son. I take it we won't have time for him to be real sociable to you or you to him. We got to get the news you all got and get it back to

Shelby and Sevier, so you tell us and we'll listen."

One by one, the men made their reports while Nate and I listened. When everyone had finished, Nate shook each man by the hand and told them, "I want you to know that I am grateful for you all keeping an eye on my family and giving them protection.

We all mounted, Nate more slowly because he was waiting to hug his wife. She gave each of us a sack of food and we were off. We rode until we reached where the army had stopped for the night and went immediately to find the colonels.

They were easy to find. They were just starting their daily conference of colonels when Nate walked in among them. Of course I was only half a step behind him.

Nate's Report

A lot of what we found out, like as not you already had figured out. So any time you need me to hurry past something, just hit my cousin Dan Bowman with something and I'll hurry.

Our spies heard or got the idea that Ferguson's main purpose was to work with Cruger and Brown to catch Clark between them and destroy Clark in the same way that Tarleton had destroyed Buford's force at the Waxhaws. To gain intelligence on Clark's whereabouts, Ferguson let a lot of his Tories visit their families with orders to report anything they heard about Clark's movements or whereabouts to him right away.

Using the information he got daily by messengers from Cruger and Brown, Ferguson tried to maneuver to be a blocking force to stop Clark and hold him for the kill. Ferguson, Cruger, and Brown were tired of Tarleton getting all the praise and glory from Cornwallis and aimed to get some themselves by using the same murdering and ruthless tactics Tarleton used on Buford's men at the Waxhaws.

Fergusons plans got changed quick when the two deserters

from Sevier's bunch caught up with him. I reckon they told Ferguson that Sevier was a bringing over three thousand men to get revenge on the British by destroying Ferguson.

Ferguson didn't waste a minute. He sent riders to Cruger, Brown, Cornwallis and about everybody else with messages that he (Ferguson) was badly outnumbered and about to be attacked. He told them he was in a serious fix and needed their help right now.

Ferguson didn't take a straight course to Cornwallis. The word we got from one spy was that he was afraid Sevier would get in front of him and ambush him. By taking a bit of a meandering route, he hoped to pick up reinforcements, round up the men he had released to visit their kinfolks and to throw Sevier off his trail. He figured Sevier will go straight to Ninety-Six to try to ambush him. Ferguson's notion was to catch Sevier between him and Cruger and Brown. Maybe Ferguson figured the three of them would be able to ambush us and with superior forces, be able to whip Sevier six ways from Sunday.

Truth to tell, I think his wandering around will make Ferguson easier to catch. If he'd just retreated like the blazes in a straight line, he'd have probably got away. Of course, if we don't watch it, he might get away anyway.

The way we had it told to us, When Ferguson left Gilbert Town, he moved his army over to the Green River region a looking for Clark. After a few days, Sevier's deserters told him that Sevier and his three thousand or so Back Water men were a coming to kill him.

Ferguson sent two men, Collins and Quinn, to tell Cornwallis what was a going on and to get some reinforcements. Collins and Quinn made some pretty good time until some Patriots got suspicious and decided to stop them. They had made pretty good time and had took the most direct route, crossing Second Broad river at Webb's Ford; then to cross the First Broad river at Stice's Shoal. From Stices Shoal, they made good time to Collins' Mill on

Buffalo. From there, they moved south-east to King's Mountain.

They were making good time, that is, until they met up with Alexander Henry at his place. Alexander is a true patriot and he paid attention to them as they ate and drank. They saw they had made him suspicious so they left in a big hurry which made Alex Henry even more suspicious. Henry sent his sons to follow Collins and Quinn. They found they were being followed by the Henry boys but now are traveling no more than eight to ten miles a day. The Henry boys have Collins and Henry treed. They won't get to Cornwallis in time for Ferguson to get help.

Ferguson also sent word to Colonel Cruger commander at Ninety-Six, telling Cruger he needed a big militia reinforcement. The message told Cruger that Ferguson needed at least several regiments of militia. The men we talked to said that Cruger don't have half the number Ferguson asked for. Ferguson then put out the word that his is on the way to Ninety-Six but the spies watching him don't believe it.

They do think that Ferguson is trying hard to capture Clark and his bunch. He has sent out a passel of spies trying to find out where Clark is camping or traveling. On Sunday, October first, Ferguson and his force stopped by Baylis Earle's place. While there, they killed and butchered a steer and burned five hundred dozen sheaves of oats.

We have had men close to Ferguson's bunch. One man was captured. His name is Andy Miller. The British were taking him with them along with another captive. Lew Musick and two of the Twitty brothers had just got back from attacking the British at Augusta, Georgia.

Lew and the Twitty Brothers, hearing of British activity in the area, decided to scout it out. We went with them. It didn't take much riding until we stopped on the main road. We stopped where we could stay hid and we could spy on the main road without being seen. I swear, it seemed that we could see the Red Coats on the road for over a mile. Looking close, we could tell for sure that Ferguson's bunch was a big part of the parade. We had a pretty good place to watch from so, having no chance to get away and bring news to you, we stayed hid and watched the long parade of Red coats.

Truth to tell, I believe there were a sight more Tories than British soldiers in the crowd. They had flankers out and seemed to be covering a lot of ground so we didn't risk getting caught trying to get around them.

After the main crowd passed, we saw a British soldier and an African slave in a cart coming up behind the bigger bunch. A horse was tied to the back of the cart. We figured they had maybe had to fix a wheel or something and had fallen behind.

While we watched, the rope holding the horse tied to the back of the cart loosened and the horse began to graze beside the road. The soldier and the slave didn't even notice that the horse was loose.

Dan slipped back to the horse and led it close to the brush and tied its rope on to a low branch. The cart made it about a hundred yards when the soldier noticed that the horse was gone.

The Red Coat began to blame the slave for the lost horse. He stopped the cart and stood up, looking over the road behind them. He finally saw the horse.

We were afraid that he would holler for help or sent the slave to fetch help but he didn't. He turned that cart around and went back to the horse. By the time he got the cart back to the horse, the tail of the column was easy a quarter mile ahead of them.

When he reached the horse, he cussed the slave and told him to tie the horse back to the cart. The slave started to do just that but when he jerked the rope, he found it wouldn't budge and called that the rope was hung on something.

It was hard not to laugh but we didn't. Dan was in the bresh where the rope was tied and I was a little ways behind him. The Twitty brothers were hid where a tree had been blowed down and still had leaves and brush enough to hide them.

The soldier jumped down off the cart, still a cussing, and pulled hard on the rope. The rope didn't budge and he didn't stop cussing.

In fact, the soldier didn't stop cussing until the Twitty boys were between him and his musket. Me'n Dan here stepped out with cocked rifles and they give up just like we asked them to do. He didn't aim to give up but our pieces were cocked and his was still in the cart. He cussed us a right smart. He sure was hell on cussing.

Now you will never guess who that Red coat we caught was. Sunday gospel truth, that Red Coat soldier was Ferguson's cook. Sunday gospel truth, he was Ferguson's cook and he was behind because he had to finish Ferguson's breakfast before he could start traveling.

Not only was the soldier Ferguson's cook, he had iron kettles with the rather large breakfast being kept warm. I reckon Ferguson must have had it in mind for a dozen to join him when he ate.

While we were looking at the food, the slave lit out a running into the bresh. I don't know where he thought he was going and I don't reckon he did either. He sure wasn't running toward the British and I know for a fact he was a runnin toward Patriots.

The cook was not riding, either on his cart or on a horse. We had him walk to see if the exercise would clean up his language a little bit. It didn't. His cussin was so funny that the two Twitty boys like to died a laughing.

Of course, we knew his loud cussin and talk was to try to get the British to hear him and rescue him. Finally, the Twitty brothers told him that if they even suspected that the British were near; suspected -- not heard or seen, just suspected, that they aimed to take two sharp knives to him. After that, he didn't do any more loud cussin or talk.

In a quiet shady place, we talked to Ferguson's cook. The first time he got uppity, Bob Twitty cut off his coat and weskit and then cut one of his braces. After that, the answers came quicker and easier.

The cook told us enough to know that the information we had on Ferguson aiming to catch Clark and his men as they made their retreat from Augusta was right. We also learned that Ferguson knew Campbell, Shelby and Sevier were after him but figured he would get help in plenty of time and was looking for a place to make a defense until he got help.

Victuals Well Dressed, An Art work by Pamela White, whitehistoricart.com. Used with artist's permission.

The Twitty brothers took all of Ferguson's breakfast and

paroled the cook. They told the cook that there were over five hundred "Back Water" men after Ferguson and they aimed to get him. The cook promised to report his parole to Ferguson and then be on parole.

Art work by Richard Luce (richardluce.com) and used with artist's permission

9

Moving to the Kill

DIARY OF Captain Alexander CHESNEY, British Army

Oct 1. At this period the North Carolina men joined us fast. Our spies returned from beyond the mountains with intelligence that the rebels were embodying rapidly. Other spies brought us word that Col. CLARKE had taken Fort Augusta with its stores, etc., on which we marched toward White Oak and Green River to intercept him on his return from Georgia. Col.

FERGUSON detached the horse in three divisions, one under my command to proceed along the Indian line until I could make out CLARKE's route, and join Captain TAYLOR at Bailey Earle Fort. I proceeded as far as Tyger river and there learning that CLARKE had gone up the banks of bushy fork of Seluda [Saluda] river, I took six of the best mounted men and got on his track until I overtook the main body and one of the enemy prisoners in view of it, whom I carried to Col. FERGUSON who thus obtained the information wanted.

Oct. 4th. Our spies from Holston, as well as some left at the Gap of the mountain brought us word that the rebel force amounted to 3,000 men; on which we retreated along the north side of the Broad river, and sent the wagons along the south side as far as the Cherokee ford, where they joined us. We marched to King's Mountain and there camped with a view of approaching Lord Cornwallis army and receiving support. By Col. FERGUSON's orders I sent express to the Militia officers to join us here ....

* * *

For the next two days, we didn't make quite as good time chasing Ferguson as we could have. I reckon that if Nate had been the only person they had listened to, there would have never been a 'battle of King's Mountain' because Ferguson would never have made it that far. The trouble was, our colonels were getting more information than you could shake a stick at and a bunch of it was flat out wrong.

There was the report that Ferguson was going just as fast as he could to Ninety-Six, which of course, he wasn't. But just because he wasn't didn't mean that the report didn't sound like it was reliable. Studying on it later, I determined that if an officer didn't have all the facts, that some of them would fill in what they didn't know with what they thought must be going on. It sure seemed foolish to me that a man would make up stuff so he could give a good sounding report but I'm sure convince that some of them done it.

Of course, Ferguson had the same trouble of figuring out what information was right and what information was a flat out lie. After I got back to camp and told the men who wondered where I'd been what I'd been up to, we had a big laugh about Ferguson.

"Men," I told them, "When this war is over, I aim to sell stock to the British with me doing the selling and them a doing the counting. That dern Ferguson is convinced there's over three thousand of us after him and hot on his trail."

Now that got a big laugh out of everybody because there was a sight less than half that number in our force. Two or three men repeated it and everybody laughed again and pounded me on the back. A few dug out jugs from somewhere and insisted I have a dram with them.

Now I wasn't a stranger to ale, wine or whiskey, but I was tired and had a little more than I was used to drinking. One thing is for sure, I slept good that night.

For the rest of the campaign, sometimes a dozen times a day, somebody would say, "I want to sell stock to the British with them a doing the counting."

Then some folks would laugh and some would tell tales about me and Nate a spying of Ferguson. The tales made it sound a whole lot more fun than it was and made me sound a whole lot smarter than I really am. Still, I guess folks have to talk about something just to make the time pass easier.

Another good thing about the news I told them was everybody

got the idea that Ferguson was a running from us because we had him scared. I aint sure he was scared but it was hard for the men to fear somebody they thought was a scared of them.

An unexpected thing happened after the men started a talking about me and Nate scouting and spying for Campbell, Shelby and Sevier. Everybody started talking it up that me'n Nate were the best scouts and spies in the whole army.

I'm here to tell you that it aint the truth but that's sure what folks were saying. It sure amazed me but the more I tried to say it wasn't so, the more folks believed to be the truth.

I knew that Nate would be by after we stopped for the night and figured that I would get him to explain it to me. I figured that he would be about as confounded as I was but hoped that between the two of us, we could figure it out.

That evening, I talked to Nate about it and he had some ideas as to why folks felt that way. Nate told me, "Dan, I believed it's because you made some of the stories so funny. The way you told about the slave running off so fast that you expected his knees to hit his head and knock him out has a lot of men laughing. Your tale about Ferguson's cook cussing so hard that everybody was laughing at him and your tale about him getting caught away from his musket sure caused the men to laugh."

"Well, I don't see how telling funny tales makes me a good spy."

"It's human nature. The men had never thought of you as either funny or as a spy. Now they think you are both."

"Well it sure beats the tar out of anything I've ever seen or heard of in my life."

"Look at it this a way, when word gets out that a man is real good at something - - - It's just naturally easier for folks to believe he is good at everything."

"It aint right."

"I didn't say it was right. I said it was human nature."

"Well I'll bet Sevier, Campbell and Shelby don't think so."

"Don't bet too much. Major McDowell just told me to find you and get ready to spy out what Ferguson is doing and where he's heading."

"What?"

"Get a few hours sleep. We go out tonight. I'll have us a bag of food."

I didn't see myself getting any sleep and figured that even if I did that it wouldn't be enough to help. It turned out that I was wrong about both figurings.

Nate woke me about five or six hours later. I wasn't sure of the time but judging from the stars it was just past midnight. In no more than fifteen or twenty minutes we were saddled up and leading our horses away from the camp full of sleeping men. Nate had us some fried cornbread that had been fried with bacon mixed into the batter.

We rode the rest of the night and arrived at Nate's farm an hour before the first sigh of dawn. Nate's son Hiram and two militiamen met us with the dogs, David and Goliath. While Hiram and I took the horses, Nate gave instructions to the two militiamen. Hiram and I weren't long with the horses, just long enough to give them feed and rub them down real good. Well maybe it did take a while but I was too tired to notice it.

We finished taking care of the horses and got back to Nate as the first three men he had sent for arrived. Fortunately, these were men who had just returned from following Ferguson. Apparently, they had been relieved of the duty the evening before.

As it turned out, there were three teams spying on Ferguson. Each would spy for a day and be relieved by another team. This team gave a good briefing but one that was confusing as to figuring out what Ferguson had on his mind.

We were told that Ferguson didn't go near as far as we had thought he would. The report we got was that he didn't begin his march until late afternoon on the second of October, and then only traveled for four hours or so. That night, he put his men in a defensive position and they all slept on their muskets all night long. The word we got was that they were underway at dawn the following day and stopped for the night at a Tory named Tate's place. From what we were told, Ferguson had traveled less than thirty-five miles in three days.

"I can't figure Ferguson out," I told Nate.

"I'm not sure I can. If he'd just kept a going in any one direction, he'd have got clean away and been with other British troops to give him support. Instead, he goes first one direction and then another."

"I'm not sure Ferguson knows what he's a doing."

Nate looked up from the map he had been figuring Ferguson's movements on and told me, "I figure that in the last six days of moving around, Ferguson is only a little more than thirty miles closer to Cornwallis. Of course, he might just be aiming to confuse us to death."

"If that's what he wants to do to us, he may well succeed. I wonder how good his spies are? If he knew how far away Sevier and Shelby were, why did he have his men sleep in a defensive line?"

"Dan, you may have just hit it. Ferguson may not have good spies. Not that it would be possible for him to have any as good as we are."

"Nate, we have word that he is camped out at Tate's place. Why camp there when he could make it to Charlotte in less than three days hard march?"

"His men and horses may be in worse shape than we know about or maybe he is expecting help to get to him before we can."

"Nate, why don't you stay here. Rest your horse and yourself. I'll take two of your neighbors and we'll ride over to Tate's and see what is going on there. When we find our something, two of us will ride like furies to tell you and you can get the news to Campbell, Sevier and Shelby on a fresh horse."

Nate didn't answer at once. I could see he was fighting with himself over what to do. He wanted a little time with his family and he didn't want to hurt our chances of getting Ferguson. Finally, he nodded.

"Dan, I'll send a message by my kin to the colonels. I'll use Rufus Bowman. The message will tell them that Ferguson is at Tate's and that we are still spying on him. That will give the colonels some idea of what to do next. I'll tell them we will let them know quickest when we get an idea of which way he will jump. They can send word back by Rufus if they want us to do anything else."

Catherine had been listening. Before we had a chance to say anything else, she handed Nate a sharp quill, ink and a scrap of paper. Nate placed them on the table and told me, "I think this will work. Now you go to Tate's and see what Ferguson is going to do to confuse us next.

"Who do you think I should take with me?"

"Take two of the Hurley boys with you. They know the country and they aint new to spying. Tell them I said Hugh and John should go with you. Hiram, take Dan over to the Hurley's place and then hurry back."

"Yes Pa."

Moments later I was mounted and following Hiram as he led

the way to the Hurley farm. Hiram led at a good pace, not a gallop but a good canter. Within half an hour we were at the Hurley place and half an hour later we were on our way to the Tate place to spy on Ferguson.

The next day, October 5th, two messengers were spied going to Tate's place with messages for Ferguson. Since sending more than one copy of the same message was usually done to make sure that that at least one copy got through. We made sure that one didn't get through by knocking the rider off his horse and taking both him and the message. The message read:

I don't see how you can possibly [defend] the country and its neighborhood that you [are] now in. The game from the mountains is just what I expected. Am glad to find you so capitally supported by the friends to government in North

Carolina. I flattered myself they would have been equal to the mountain lads, and that no further call for the defensive would have been [made] on this part of the Province. I begin to think our views for the present rather large.

The next trick we pulled was to waylay the messenger after he had left Ferguson. Hugh and John Hurley told the messenger that his only chance of living was to tell them everything that he knew of Ferguson's plans. To get the man's attention, Hugh drug up a pig by its back legs. Since the messenger didn't seem too impressed, John took out his knife and ran it over his sharpening stone for a minute. He then took the knife and shaved a little of the messenger's stubble from his face. He then hit the knife blade a few more licks on the sharpening stone. Making sure he had the messenger's attention, he castrated the pig.

I aint sure who squalled the loudest, the pig or the messenger. One thing was for dern sure, the messenger had no idea of keeping any secrets after that pig was castrated. Not only did the messenger answer every question he was asked. He was volunteering information faster than we could write it down. He told us that Ferguson was on his way to a high hill that he called Little King's Mountain. He also let us know, without being asked, that Ferguson expected to be reinforced at Little King's Mountain.

The messenger was also carrying a letter from Ferguson to *Cornwallis that read:*

"I am on my march towards you, by a road leading from Cherokee Ford, north of Kings Mountain. Three or four hundred good soldiers, part dragoons, would finish the business. Something must be done soon. This is their last push in this quarter, they are since joined by Clarke and Sumpter.

Well that part was sure a new one on me. If Sevier had been joined by Clark and Sumter, I sure didn't know anything about it. Well Cruger had already told Ferguson that he couldn't provide any help. This told me that Ferguson wanted to set up defense works on the Little King's Mountain and wait to be reinforced. I didn't figure Sevier and Campbell and Shelby would give them that much time.

It wasn't that we didn't have room to worry. I didn't doubt for a minute that Ferguson didn't have more organized and well supplied as well as well armed reinforcements close by that we did. Cornwallis had Tarleton, Cruger, Brown and others ready to come when they were called. This doesn't even count all the British soldiers in Charleston and Savannah.

If you got right down to it, the British had forts or operations set up at Cheraw, Camden, Carey's Fort, Manigault's Ferry, Fort Watson, Georgetown, Nelson's Ferry, Monck's Corner, Fort Dorchester, 15 Mile House, Stono Fort, Fair Lawn Plantation, 10 Mile House, Wappetaw Church, Quarter House, Fort Pleasant, Fort Arbuthnot, Fort Johnson, Beaufort, Barton's Post, Hudson's Ferry,

Fort Balfour, Fort Galphin, Fort Ninety-Six, Rocky Mount, Belleville and Hanging Rock.

It was un-telling how many soldiers the British had in the Carolina's. I was pretty sure that Cornwallis had soldiers in North Carolina. Thinking it over, I figured we had better hit Ferguson before he got a lot of help from a lot of places.

I had been told that there were more American Patriots in Fort Pleasant as prisoners than there were in the American army in the Carolinas. I didn't know for sure but some folks were convinced that was the truth.

The more I studied about the messages we had taken from the British, the more I became convinced that both Ferguson and Cruger figured that Ferguson had a tough fight on his hands. As I saw it, Ferguson figured he could win and Cruger either didn't think they could win or Cruger didn't want to share any glory with Ferguson or any other British officer. I could a been wrong but that is how I figured it.

Somewhere, probably just from having time to set and rest and think, it come to me that the British Looked at war and fighting a sight different from the way we did. We were used to being ready for attacks from the Chickamauga. We were used to getting tired of being the ones waiting to be attacked and going out to attack them first. Traveling on short provisions was not unusual for us and neither was having to fight without some officer telling us what to do and how to do it.

I reckoned that if we were more like the British, we would have already been whipped. Just look at the whole thing - - - at everything that had happened in the past six months or so. Charlestown had fallen with between five thousand and six thousand men taken captives. Most of these men were now prisoners at Fort Pleasant. Before we had a chance to get over that setback, Tarleton had murdered men who were trying to surrender at the Waxhaws. Then General Granny Gates had wasted good men at the battle of Camden and had retreated the fastest of any of them. Tom Sumter's men had been scattered Tories were now trying to steal everything that wasn't nailed down and murdering patriots for their property.

I wondered that, maybe if Major Patrick Ferguson hadn't sent his warning over the mountain, we would have stayed there and made ready for winter. It sure wasn't in our nature to draw back from any challenge to a fight. We might have stayed where we were and waited to see what happened.

We had good leaders. Shelby, Sevier, Cleveland, Campbell and others were good not just because they could bellow out orders. They were good because any one of them would sacrifice personal advancement for the good of the army. Campbell was in the post of overall leader but a daily council of the colonels decided which way that we would jump. I don't reckon I ever heard of any of them getting a bad case of the big head.

Another thing that crossed my mind was ability or rather how a man's ability could place him in charge of other men. I couldn't think of a time I had followed a man just because of his being an officer. The officers we followed had proven themselves more than just a few times. They continued to prove and improve themselves.

They were respected leaders but they seem to show a lot of confidence in us, the men they led. I remembered what we had been told, "Men, when we meet the enemy, don't wait for orders. Each one of you be your own officer, and do the very best you can. Take every care you can. give yourselves of every advantage that you can. In the woods, shelter yourselves, and give them Indian play! Move from tree to tree. Press the enemy! Kill all you can. Your officers will not run from danger. We will be with you! Fight hard! Be alert."

Well, I was satisfied that we could do all that. All that and more. Not because we were natural born leaders because we weren't. Not because we loved to fight because, for the most part, we didn't.

The truth was, we had been taught our duty all of our lives. Not so much a duty to a country as a duty to our kin and neighbors. Part of that duty was to make sure we weren't pushed around or allowed our kin and neighbors to be pushed around.

One remedy to having to put up with bad laws without fighting was moving out of reach of the bad laws. Not all, but some of the 'overmountain' people settled there after the regulator movement failed at Alamance.

There were really two separate regulator movements. One was in North Carolina and the other in South Carolina. As I understood it, both fracases were because the folks got the idea that the government and law were there only to benefit those with riches who lived in the coastal regions of the two colonies.

The western areas of South Carolina were plagued by outlaw bunches that did much as they pleased. They got away with their outlawry because there were no courts or law to protect the people. The movement in South Carolina began in 1767 and was led by leading planters supported by law abiding farmers to regulate or manage laws and enforcing laws in the western areas of South Carolina. This group resolved to manage or regulate the areas society.

The South Carolina regulators arrested and tried criminals. They set up courts to hear and rule on arguments and disputes. Furthermore, they took their complaints to the assembly and governor of South Carolina.

The South Carolina regulators presented their complaints in a civil manner to both the colonial assembly and the royal governor. The colonial government allowed that the complaints had justification and provided six courts districts to the western region of South Carolina. This action solved the problems and the Regulators were able to quit and leave government duties to the colony.

The Regulator movement is North Carolina was for different

reasons but happened about the same time. Small farmers didn't like the cheating and blackmailing being done by sheriffs and courts. These people asked or petitioned the colonial government of North Carolina to get rid of the corrupt sheriffs and courts. The assembly of the colony of North Carolina agreed but the royal governor, the courts and the provincial council didn't agree and the corruption continued.

The Regulator movement began as a peaceful and orderly change but violence began when corrupt officials went free without punishment. Violent acts caused many people to move away from the regulation and the Regulators were routed at Alamance Creek in May, 1761. Seven regulators were hung and the movement was ended. Like I said, a group of the Regulators moved west and helped form the Watauga Association. Some decided to submit things stayed tense between the farmers of western North Carolina and the uppity tidewater big wigs.

I wondered how much the Regulator movements had to do with the revolt against England. I hadn't heard it said that there was a connection but I kind of thought there might be a connection. One thing for sure, it taught folks how to organize and plan a sight better than they had before.

I wondered if the British soldiers would have the will to fight us if they lost their leaders. I didn't think so but I had no real proof. I wondered if the Tories who now were so intent to steal from their Patriot neighbors and murder them. I didn't know but I was a bit ashamed of how folks who once were neighbors and friends could now be enemies.

For my part, I was strongly convinced of the justness of our cause but I wondered if the Tories were just as strongly convinced that their cause was the one that was just and right. Thinking of 'Bloody Banastre Tarleton' and Tarleton's quarter, I made up my mind that no matter what, I would not surrender.

10

King's Mountain

Nate with a handful of his kinfolk and neighbors rode up to join me before noon. I was glad to see them and to have a few more fighting men with me. Nate tossed me a bundle that I was glad to find held food.

"Catherine is afraid that I'll let you starve if she don't help."

"She's probably right. I'm glad to see you all."

"You'll have more company soon. Jim Williams and nearly five hundred South Carolina militiamen are meeting Campbell and your bunch at the Cowpens. Our colonels got together and decided that around nine hundred men on the best horses are traveling fast to hit Ferguson before he gets away or gets reinforced. We should be fighting no later than tomorrow or the next day."

"Is that good?"

"Good or not, it will happen soon. I reckon we can handle it."

"We'll do it."

"I reckon you have figured out exactly where we are a going to whip Ferguson."

"I reckon."

"Well I'll be derned. Where?"

"The last I heard, Ferguson is camped on top of a mountain - - - or rather a hill, King's Mountain."

"Well, is it a hill or a mountain?"

"We overmountain men wouldn't call it a mountain. We'd call it a hill."

"No matter what it's called, after the next day or two, folks may call it bloody."

"So what do we do now?"

"We send word to Campbell and keep on Ferguson's trail. We can start by seeing this King's Mountain hill of yours to see if Ferguson is there."

"That sounds easy enough."

Nate called over two men and had them change to fresh horses. He gave them a message telling them that Ferguson was believed to be on top of King's Mountain. The men checked the horses' shoes, bridles and saddles. I hoped the horses appreciated how serious the men were. I guess it was time for folks to start being real serious.

I wasn't afraid, or maybe I was afraid. It's hard to say. I knew that I could be killed or be bad hurt in a matter of hours or days. I knew that the British were not giving quarter and were bragging on what fate wounded or captured Patriots could expect.

I didn't want to be captured, wounded or killed. That being said, the thought of leaving the fight to others didn't cross my mind. I felt my gut draw in real tight and I said a quick prayer. I thought of Sally and of how soft and warm her lips felt on mine. I wanted to feel them again. I shivered a bit, took a deep breath and let it out slow.

Nate clapped his hand on my back and shook me a bit.

"We're going to be good. I been through these fights before."

"Yeah."

"Know one thing I figured out?"

"No. What?"

"I never think about Catherine until the fight is over and done with. Ever man I knowed that went into a fight like this thinking of his woman didn't come out whole. It's best to maybe write a few words and leave it with somebody. When you come out of the battle, you take it back and send it if you want. Of course, after the fight, you can always burn it."

"Yeah, I'll do that."

"Oh! You mean to tell me that you got a woman?"

"I hope so. I think so. I mean I left in such a hurry that I didn't say goodbye."

"Let me get this straight, Dan, you didn't say goodbye?"

"That's right."

"So you left without her a carrying on and crying and begging you not to go?"

"Yes."

"She didn't have a chance to make you go all wobbly in the knees and want to say anything so she would stop crying and carrying on?"

"She didn't."

"Dan, you're a sharper man than I thought."

"What?"

"You got it made. You just tell her you had to hurry so as not to get left. Tell her you wrote her a letter but couldn't find nobody to take it to her. Of course, you'll have to have a letter to give her then."

"You don't mean to tell me that Catherine acts like that when you got to leave do you?"

"Not after the first time or two, she don't."

"What happened?"

"Well, Catherine commenced to sobbing and crying and a begging me not to go. She was getting me all tore up. Then her mama pulled her off a me and like to shook her hair right off her. Her mama told her that a man going to battle didn't need to be a thinking about his woman at home a pissing tears about him a being gone to do battle. She told her that was the easiest way to get a man killed and besides, damned if she aimed to listen to her moaning and squalling. Then she told me to get the hell out and damned if she would put up with a son-in-law who would allow such carrying on from his woman. You can bet that when she pulled Catherine off and shoved her away from me that I lit a shuck out of there."

"Lord a mercy!"

"It's a fact. Listening to a woman a carrying on can get a man killed deadern being struck by lightning."

"So I reckon I shouldn't be thinking about Sally?"

"Sure you can, if you want to get killed right quick."

"So I reckon I won't be thinking about Sally."

"Sounds like a good idea to me."

"I reckon it is. With what we are a going into, we don't need to have any distractions."

I studied over what Nate had told me and asked, "I reckon you know a right smart about women?"

"No man does. If ary man says he does, he's either fooling himself or lying to you."

"It seems like it's a hard job to me, especially if a man can't understand them."

"The funny thing is, me and your pa had almost this same talk ---- it must a been twenty year ago --- with your grandpa. He gave us some advice that we both followed ever since."

Seeing that Nate wasn't aiming to volunteer the advice they had been given, I asked, "I don't expect you remember what the advice was . . .?"

"Oh yes, I remember."

"And the advice was . . . ?"

"The advice was to never argue with a woman, always agree with a woman, and always do what you have to do --- If the woman asks why, just tell you made a mistake. It might seem a little foolish but it keeps a man out of a sight of trouble and it works."

I might not have found anything about the mysteries of women but I learned one thing for sure. I learned that spying on an enemy could wear a man down. It wasn't as wearing as chopping wood but it was wearing.

In the first place, Nate insisted that a messenger go find the rest of the overmountain bunch at least every three hours. Every three hours and that was if nothing had changed. Changes would be cause a messenger to leave right off. After 30 hours, our spy bunch had gone from thirty-two men down to twelve.

Spying was not easy work. We had to see the enemy without

being seen. We had to either go without a fire or keep it so small that no one could see the smoke. We had to meet up to talk about what we had seen and then get right back to spying.

It was late morning or early afternoon on October 27th and Nate had just sent out two messengers with reports for Colonels Campbell, Shelby and Sevier. It wasn't twenty minutes before one of them came a tearing back.

"They're almost here boys. Around a thousand of them. They say they been in the saddle nearly two days. It won't take long. The fight'll commence directly."

Nate rushed over and grabbed the horses bridle and the rider slid out of the saddle and told him, "Talk. What did you find out?"

"Not much, I left in a hurry. There's nigh a thousand of them some that come up from down in South Carolina. They say they've been traveling for two days and want to whip Ferguson so they can rest."

Nate drew an outline of King's Mountain in the dirt. He marked twelve points around the mountain. He then pointed at twelve men, one at a time and to the point he wanted them to go. Everyone left in a hurry. Then he nodded toward our horses and we went to meet the approaching army.

This picture depicts the 1776 attack on Charlestown. During this attack, the British tried to sail into the harbor but could not get past Fort Moultrie. Picture is a public domain print from Dover Publishing.

A depiction of Colonel William Campbell. Public Domain print from dover Publishing.

The death of Baron De Kalb at the battle of Camden. De Kalb's Maryland 'Continental Line' was possibly the only positive American fighting force at the battle. Public Domain Photo from Dover Publishing.

This print depicts the manner in which many British soldiers, their mercenary comrades and Tory loyalists treated helpless women and children whose husbands and fathers were suspected or known to be patriots. Public Domain art from Dover Publishing.

Colonel John Sevier, Portrait probably painted after he became the first governor of the new state of Tennessee.   Public Domain Print from Dover Publishing.

Isaac Shelby after he became the first governor of Kentucky. Public domain print from Dover Publications.

A young patriot prepares to leave to do his duty. Public Domain print from Dover Publishing.

Overmountain men getting ready to attack Ferguson's force on King's Mountain. Public Domain Print from Dover Publishing.

Death of Ferguson, a Public Domain print from Dover Publishing clip art.

General Horatio Gates, Once considered to replace Washington, he was disgraced after his rapid retreat from the Battle of Camden. Public Domain print from Dover Publishing.

Major Patrick Ferguson. Painting by Robert W. Wilson. Original painting was in color. Used with permission of the Artist.

The original painting of the scene above was accomplished by the Artist and 23 year Army Air Corps and USAF Veteran, Robert W. Wilson. The original painting is in the South Carolina State House.

The original color print, Victuals in Good Order, was accomplished by Pamela White, whitehistoricart.com I am obliged to the artists for allowing the use their art in this book.

Victory at King's Mountain by Richard Luce. Original print is in color. Used with artist's permission.

11

The Battle of King's Mountain

We found Shelby and the army in about twenty minutes. I reckon that Nate could have rode up to any colonel and reported but he chose Shelby. Sevier, Campbell, Cleveland and a man some said was Williams came riding up to join Shelby. Shelby had dismounted so he could stretch and the others joined Shelby on the ground.

While they waited to speak to Nate, I looked over the other men and the horses. I could tell right off that I wasn't the only man who had missed sleep. We had heard that the force had been whittled down to the nine hundred best horses and I reckon it was so, but even the best get tired and lame. With a quick count, I came up with nine hundred mounted men and maybe two hundred fifty that were a foot. There were some men there that I was sure I had never seen before. I was later told that we had been joined by some men from Georgia and some from South Carolina.

Shelby waited for Nate to finish drinking before he started his questions.

"Where's Ferguson?"

"Straight ahead on top of a hill called King's Mountain. It looked like Ferguson has posted his men on the top from one end to the other. They don't seem to be aiming to retreat. In fact, I don't think they know how close you are to them. They are set up real military though. They have sentry's posted and look prepared."

"Are the soldiers Tory militia or Regulars?"
"Maybe both. Some of them looked well trained. Some of them were

going through bayonet drills."

"How many men are there?"

"Near as we could count twelve hundred. There would be more but a bunch left to forage for supplies."

"Is there a cleared and visible path to the top of King's Mountain?"

"No. Quite a bit of trees and brush."

"That may help."

Now me, I'd have rather fought British Regulars than folks who were once our neighbors but neither we, nor they, had a lot of choice in the matter. I never really figured out why some folks were still Tory and supported the king. I suspect that it could have just been habit for a lot of them. Still, I guess some of them actually believed in what they were doing and some were hoping to gain wealth and property for their efforts.

I figured that some of the Tories just didn't like war and blamed the war on Whigs and Patriots. To those folks, submitting to the arrogance of British rule would not have hurt.

Then again, I had to figure that some folks were just flat out ignorant. They had no idea what we were fighting for or what we wanted to build. Along with these folks were Tories who were too afraid of any other form of government than what they already knew. Still others were honestly afraid of self-government and any government that didn't have the king's approval.

Of course, some Tories were sure that their sticking to the king would bring them riches and raise them up to a higher class. I didn't see that happening but I reckon some Tories counted on it.

It's a sight what some folks will do for a bit of riches.

Unfortunately, some Tories were nothing but pure outlaws. They led or rode with bands or bunches of men who were only intent of stealing from patriots and murdering patriots when it was convenient. These men had always been outlaws and used the war as an excuse to raid and steal from honest folks. These men had never been worth the air they breathed and never would, no matter what they called themselves.

Nate had scratched an outline of King's Mountain in the dirt. He was busy showing where Ferguson had placed his supplies, tents and men. Then Shelby, Campbell, Sevier and the rest of the colonels got together and talked it over.

The upshot of all the scratching in the dirt and talk was the plan of attack. Shelby, Campbell and the rest put all the men into two groups. The plan was for each group to attack from opposite sides of King's Mountain.

The plan called for Campbell take his Virginians across the south tip of the ridge, and the south easterly side. While he was getting in place, Sevier would lead his men along with McDowell's and Winston's men to move to the right side northeast of where Campbell would be attacking from. Winston would move a portion of his men to prevent any escape attempt by Ferguson.

Shelby would lead his men to the left of King's Mountain right across from Campbell. Shelby would be forming the left center and meet up with Campbell to form a line of attack. I'm not sure how all the rest formed up. It seemed like a good plan. Nate and me, we followed Shelby.

Before we got started, Shelby and the other colonels told us that we were about to fight a fight that could change everything from this day to all the days that came after. He told us we were going into a noble fight and that we should fight like heroes and not to retreat unless it was absolutely necessary. He told us to only retreat as far as we had to and to attack again as quick as we could.

I reckon that the other commanders were a telling their men the same thing. Campbell came by and told us that if any of us, men or officers, were afraid, to just leave and go home. Campbell told us that he didn't want any man who was too scared to fight to be with him.

Of course, there were none who would admit to being that scared. Scared was one thing. Showing cowardice by running off was another.

Campbell finished by telling us he was not going to quit and would fight for a week if he had to fight that long. We had been told not to yell or cheer lest we let Ferguson know where we were so we didn't. Instead we did the best we could to get ready.

We all checked our rifles, our pouches and all our cutting weapons. Quite a few of the men took off their hats and lay them with the other gear they were not taking into the battle. Instead of the hats which they feared would catch on branches and brush, they tied sashes or kerchiefs around their heads.

Then the columns started to move. We were tired, sore and hungry but we were moving to attack Ferguson and we felt pretty good about it.

When we began to move, we moved away from the plan as quick as we were moving toward Ferguson. Both the left and right wings found going a sight slower than they had planned. I found out later that Winston and his men traveled about a mile and found their view blocked by a high hill. They had no idea which way they were supposed to go. They had lost sight of the other two columns and no longer could see King's Mountain. Two riders rode up to Winston and told him they were to dismount, tie their horses and climb the hill. This caused a delay because King's Mountain was still a mile further. When the mistake was discovered, Winston and his men rushed back to their horses, remounted and rode toward King's Mountain like the devil was a chasing them.

Campbell's bunch and Shelby's had better luck. We kept quiet. We were hidden by the woods and brush until we got within four or five hundred yards of the base of King's Mountain. We had taken the picket watching for such an attack without firing a shot or letting them get a messenger off to Ferguson. It was as easy as Nate had said it would be.

Then things started to happen real quick. First there were shouts as we were first seen followed by the sound of drums beating and a shrill whistle being blown. Through the branches and brush, we could see Ferguson's men spreading out to defensive positions. They seemed to be well led and not at all panicked. Thinking on it, the fact is they seemed to have a good idea of what they were doing.

Well, we knew what we were doing too. If some of us weren't sure, we knew that all we had to do was follow Isaac Shelby and the rest of our colonels. We knew that we were attacking the man who had threatened to come over the mountains with "fire and sword," and the men that he led. We knew that we had to win because we did not expect to receive anything but "Tarleton's quarter" if we tried to surrender.

The very nature of the enemy we fought was reminded to all of us with the password we were given. The password was Buford. A grim reminder of what happened to Buford's men at the Waxhaws when they asked for quarter.

They had received Tarleton's quarter, death.

Ferguson's men fired in our direction. I don't know why because we were out of range but one man fired and his lone shot was immediately followed by a deafening volley of what seemed to be hundreds of muskets and rifles.

With "Tarleton's quarter" in mind, we moved to attack.

"Hold your fire, hold your fire! Advance! Advance!"

Shelby's command kept some of our bunch for firing back. Of course at the distance we were from the enemy, firing would have been a waste of time, powder and lead. Still, being fired at and not shooting back rubbed a bunch of our men the wrong way.

"Hold your fire, hold your fire! Until we have range!"

"Damn them, I want to shoot back," shouted one of our men.

"Keep moving. Don't waste your shots. Wait until we can hit something!"

"Damn."

Shelby kept his head and control, replying "I want every man to press on to your places, and then your fire will not be lost."

We pressed on to our places but we then heard firing from Campbell's position. We later learned that he had taken off his coat, thrown it over a limb and shouted to his men, "Yonder they are, let's get them. Yell like hell and fight like devils!"

Between the yelling and the almost constant firing as Campbell's men found targets, it was louder, and worse, than the worst thunder storm over the Smokey's that I had ever heard.

I found myself charging up the hill along with all the rest. I didn't fire, I just ran toward the enemy. The British had fired and were reloading. Their next volley seemed to go over our heads and did not damage that I could see. We kept on moving toward them, yelling our fool heads off.

By that time there was shouting from every side of King's Mountain. I reckon if shouting could have won a battle, we'd have had it won. (We later learned from captured Tories that their officers remembered Musgraves Mill and the shouting there with a right smart of concern.)

We had just got a good start on the hill when the Virginians jumped square dab into the mix.

Major Micajah Lewis, his brother, Captain Joe Lewis, and Captain Andy Colvill led Virginia militia up the mountain. According to the plan, they were to run their horses halfway up the mountain and destroy or run off the red coats advance troops. They were then supposed to fall back, leave their horses behind and join the other men in their advance up the mountain. The plan sounded real good but I guess the British didn't realize what they were supposed to do.

The British didn't get run off like they were supposed to do. They stood and fired volleys at the Virginians. The Virginians then commenced hollering like a bunch of half-drunk Chickamauga and rushing at the British line.

Here a right smart of heavy firing commenced and continued. Some of the British retreated and were killed while retreating, but the Virginians lost men too. Still the battle continued.

I finally stopped behind a tree, leveled my rifle, picked out a target and fired. To this day, I can't describe how I felt when I saw him drop. It was a feeling that wasn't all good and wasn't all bad at the same time.

After I fired, I saw that others were reloading from the cover of trees and brush. The British on top of King's mountain were able to keep up their level of fire. Of course, as long as we were behind a tree, it didn't matter how many volleys they fired.

"They are well trained and well led."

Until he spoke, I didn't know that Nate was so close. Looking toward the sound of his voice, I saw him sheltered behind a tree to my left. Like me, he was reloading his rifle.

Reloading a long-barreled rifle without exposing an arm or a shoulder was quite a trick. Not twenty feet from me, a man unloosed a string of cussing when a British musket ball clipped the exposed butt of his rifle. For some reason, his rifle being hit and his cussing seemed funny to those who saw what happened.

"What do you think Nate?"

"I think we keep trying to get closer 'til we have to turn back."

"Turn back?"

"If they charge with bayonets and we are unloaded, we will have to turn back. Not for long but we will have to turn back."

Without saying it, Nate had reminded me of a disadvantage of depending on a long rifle. While a smooth barreled Brown Bess could be loaded and fired two to four times a minute, I rifle couldn't be reloaded so fast.

The rifling in the barrels made it impossible to properly load and fire even two rounds a minute. After firing just a few shots, the rifle's barrel would be so fouled by spent black powder that reloading became slower and more difficult. Some of us used lead balls that were a little undersized with thicker greased patches to try to get a few more shots before cleaning the barrel became necessary.

"How far will we turn back?"

"Until enough of us get reloaded to do some damage. They can't move us too far because we have men all around this hill. If they give us gaps, some of our men will be able to get through the gaps and behind them."

"I hadn't thought of that."

Truth is, I had forgotten about the other column and the other points of attack. I had almost forgot about any man who was not in plain sight. I finished reloading as Nate and others finished. Without a command, we moved from behind the shelter and started back up the hill. We started back up the powder smoke covered hill known as King's Mountain.

Some of the men I'd forgotten about were having their own troubles. Cleveland and his bunch, were slowed up considerable by a stretch of soaked, swampy ground. They had no sooner got out of the swamp than they ran into Ferguson's advance guard.

I reckon that it then that Colonel Cleveland showed why he is a leader. He kept urging his men on saying "We beat the Tories before, we'll beat them again. We'll beat them today."

Riding among his men he encouraged them, "These Tories are cowards. They aint real men. If they were real men, they would be beside us!" Follow me and fight!" Remember, you are all officers! Fire as fast as you can! Stand your ground! Use trees for cover! You can retreat but don't run off!"

While his men stopped the threat from Ferguson's advance guard, Cleveland continued his fiery speeches. His men seemed to be inspired because they cheered and moved forward.

"If we have to move back, we will move back. We won't run. We will fight! If we have to move back we will, but then we will fight. We won't give up! Any man afraid to fight can leave right now!"

I was told that one man volunteered to stay behind to hold the horses but that his brother continued the fight with Cleveland and the rest. With a great will, they charged up King's Mountain. The few survivors of Ferguson's advance guard fleeing ahead of Cleveland's men.

I can't remember the name of the man who volunteered to take care of the horses. I reckon that he did a good job though. At least I didn't hear that he didn't do a good job.

It was Campbell's Virginians that got the first bayonet charge. Their path of attack was, I reckon, the roughest one any of us had to take. It was rougher, it was steeper, and it had fewer trees to take shelter behind. None of that bothered Campbell's Virginians.

Those Virginians made their way up until they were almost at the top of the hill. Just when it looked like they could go through Ferguson's men like salts through a goose, Ferguson ordered his rangers to charge them with bayonets. Some of the Virginians unwisely stood their ground until some were bayoneted. They then began their retreat back down the hill. Some were overtaken and killed but the British broke off their charge before they were too far separated from their line. Some of Campbell's men retreated to the top of the next ridge where Campbell and his officers got control of them again.

Colonel Campbell and two of his officers took position halfway between the Virginians and Ferguson. There they hollered for their Virginians to join them in attacking Ferguson. A loud cheer roared out of the Virginians as they moved to join their commander.

I was later told that even Virginians who had been wounded joined the attack. I never had any cause to doubt the Virginians courage.

While the Virginians were attacking, being forced back and attacking again, Shelby's bunch were raising as much dust as we could. The whole top of the mountain seemed to be a mess of flame and powder smoke.

While Campbell and his Virginians were attacking, retreating and attacking; Shelby had us push our attack from our side of the hill. "Get 'em men! Remind 'em that they got to contend with us!"

We charged right up that hill onward toward the British line. It's a fact that they British were paying more attention to the bayonet charge against Campbell than they were us but that didn't last long. While we pushed and pulled our way up, firing with good effect as we moved, we got their attention.

Just like before, a long whistle blast followed by a more loud blasts from the whistle were heard over the gunfire and the bayonet charge was called back. We didn't have a chance to overrun their line. Moving as steady as if they were in a parade, the British turned a bayonet charge on us. Nate was right. No matter how brave we were, we couldn't face bayonet steel with empty rifles. Again, we were forced to retreat. We retreated but we retreated in good order, we reloaded and fired as we moved away from the line of bayonets. We stopped when we got to the bottom and waited for Shelby to give us orders.

"Reload boys! Reload quick!"

"We'll get 'em Shelby!" I don't know who answered Shelby's commands but it just encouraged him.

"Get 'em loaded boys. Load and get to the top of the hill. Get up there and give them a hell of a fire!"

"We'll give 'em hellfire! Lead us up there Shelby!"

It didn't take us no more than fifteen minutes to the top of the hill again. We made good time taking ground but bayonets forced us to retreat again. I'm not sure whether we had to retreat two or three times. It didn't matter because the enemy lost men every time we moved on them. They lost more when they faced us with a bayonet charge. I don't reckon that they ever had a chance.

No! They didn't have a chance. We fired at them from the

cover of the tree line while they fired in formation from the crest of the hill with no cover. When they made bayonet charges, they were forced out of formation by the brush and trees that offered us protection.

Our best shots, men like Josh Culbertson were put up high where they could fire at the British. They fired and most every time they fired, an enemy died.

We lost men too. Colonel Shelby's brother, Moses, was wounded twice.

Like Shelby's attacks, the other parts of our army attacked, retreated and attacked again. Every time we attacked, the enemy lost men. Every time we retreated, the enemy lost men. Of course, we lost men too. The good thing was, we didn't lose near as many men as the British lost.

To hear me a telling this, you might get the idea that I knew everything that was a going on while it was going on. I didn't. Truth is, I only knew what was right beside me or right in front of me - - - and I might a missed some of that.

Like the first time we retreated, there were two of Ferguson's men who seemed bound and determined to get me. They didn't, of course but that's what it seemed like. When we stopped retreating and made our attack, it seemed like they were doing their best to stop me. Of course they didn't stop me but that's what it seemed like.

I saw the trees that I sheltered behind and I saw the faces above the Brown Bess muskets that shot at me. During all the battle, I had no idea of tactics or strategy. I only knew the men beside me and the men shooting at me.

It was only after the battle, when I talked to and listened to other men that I got a bigger idea of what had happened. During the battle, I charged and retreated with the rest and fired when I thought I had a shot. I didn't think we would lose but I don't reckon I'd have bet I would live to see the battle won.

A lot of men I talked to felt the same. I've told you why I thought the Tories fought for the king. I reckon we patriots fought for independence because we couldn't abide being looked down on or treated as a lesser man.

Our side wasn't the only one with good marksmen. The Tories had some too and some were armed with rifles. They were a deadly bunch and hid behind a chain of rocks. From their hiding places, they kept up a steady fire at our men. Shelby decided it had to be stopped.

To stop it, Shelby sent Ensign Robert Campbell, of the Virginians, to shake the hidden Tory shooters out of hiding. They went up at a pretty good clip and were close enough to hit the British with rocks when a bayonet charge forced some of us to fall back.

Campbell didn't fall back. I reckon that he figured he had worked too hard to get where he was to leave. He had his men take cover and keep on fighting from on top of the hill.

After his men were set up and could cover each other, Robert Campbell went to help Colonel Campbell get his men set up to attack again. While they were getting set to charge up the hill again, the Virginians he had left kept things on top of King's Mountain hot with their rifle fire. This caused the British to pull in to a smaller area and help the men behind the rocks.

By the time Campbell was ready to move again, the fight was going on at just about every point around King's Mountain. I heard Bailie Peyton later say that "the mountain appeared volcanic; there flashed along its summit, and around its base, and up its sides, one long sulphurous blaze." Well I aint never seen a volcano and I don't know that Bailie has either but the way he described it was likely right. There was powder smoke everywhere. Everyone I saw had black powder smudges on their hands and faces.

One thing for dern sure, it was loud. The gun fire, officers from both sides shouting commands, men a hollering and whooping at each other and the enemy - - - it was loud. Sometimes we could hear the shrill squeal that we knew was Ferguson blowing his whistle. Worse yet, we could hear the moans of our wounded. As we closed on the top of the hill, we could hear the British wounded.

It was then that colonel and his South Carolina boys jumped into the fracas. The South Carolina boys had served under Sumter and they wanted to win another one. I heard that one of them retreated but I can't say for sure.

All of us, every man was pushing hard to get a victory. We wanted to show the British that we weren't all as easy to whip as Gates had been at Camden. Even when bayonet charges forced us back, we knew we would charge again and that we would win.

Some said Shelby's men had the roughest time but me and Nate figured that Campbell's men did. It's hard to say but when the smoke cleared, I was sure that Ferguson and his bunch had the roughest time. But the smoke hadn't cleared yet.

Robert Campbell led a charge and, before it was over, killed the man who led Ferguson's rangers. Another of Campbell's officers, Will Edmondson, rushed right into the thickest part of the fight and then fought his way out. After firing his rifle, Will reloaded and fired, killing one of the British. Then Will used his rifle as a club to knock away the Brown Bess musket of another of the enemy. He then grabbed the man by the neck and dragged him back to Campbell's line. During the next charge, Will was fatally wounded and died after the battle.

Colonel Campbell was one battling Scot! Leading a charge with his ancestors' claymore held up high and yelling encouragement to his men, Campbell inspired his men to fight.

Our different groups charged, fell back and moved up again. Every time we did, it was against fewer enemy. It goes without saying that we lost good men too.

Chronicle and Hambright led their bunch of South Fork boys up the second steepest part of King's Mountain, the north-east side. Chronicle had just hollered of his men to move up when he was shot dead. Other officers stepped up and the attack continued. They continued on until a bayonet charge forced them to fall back.

I reckon that every bunch we had fought a good fight at King's Mountain. When one man was so badly wounded that they feared he would die, he gave another his rifle and pouch to continue the fight. I reckon there were more brave deeds done in the time it took to end the battle than I can remember.

Some of our men began to recognize former neighbors and friends who were on the other side. Tom Robertson was sheltered by a tree when he heard a familiar voice call his name. When he looked to see who called, he saw a Tory who had been his neighbor. The Tory shot at him but missed. Tom shot at the Tory and hit him through the lungs. When the Tory begged for help, Tom paid him no mind. He just reloaded his rifle and continued the fight.

There's one tale that two brothers on the different sides shot each other and that both died. I don't remember their name but more than one person witnessed it.

Truth is, I only saw what was right in front of me and I can't guarantee I saw all of that. I heard a lot of men talk later and from what all they had to say, a right smart happened that I didn't know about.

I remember the last time we had to fall back that some of Ferguson's men hollered to us that 'Bloody' Tarleton had arrived. I didn't pay it no mind but it made a sight of people nervous. I heard later than Sevier went around calming people down.

The last time we fell back, some of us fell back with loaded rifles. Nate hollered out "Look men, the rebels are running off."

When the British started returning to their lines, we aimed our loaded rifles and did a right smart of damage to the men with bayonets. We then began moving back up the hill, firing from behind trees as we moved. With Campbell's bunch and Shelby's bunch both moving up the hill called King's Mountain, Ferguson had a hard job whether he wanted or not.

I remember that Shelby hollered out, "Don't shoot 'til you see an enemy, and never see an enemy, without bringing him down."

We sure done it. We saw 'em, we shot 'em, we brought 'em down.

We charged right up that hill onward toward the British line. It's a fact that the British were paying more attention to the bayonet charge against Campbell than they were us but that didn't last long. While we pushed and pulled our way up, we were firing with good effect as we moved. Our firing was so good it soon got their attention.

Directly, a long whistle blast followed by a bunch more called the bayonet charge back and before we could over run them, the British turned a bayonet charge on us. I saw then what Nate had meant. We were brave but we had to back up and pull foot against the bayonet charge. We retreated but we retreated in good order, firing as we moved away from the line of bayonets. When we got to the bottom, Shelby got control of us right away.

"Reload boys! Reload quick!"

"We'll get 'em Shelby!" I don't know who answered Shelby's

commands but it just encouraged him.

"Get 'em loaded boys. Load and get to the top of the hill. Get up there and give them a hell of a fire!"

"We'll give 'em hellfire! Lead us up there Shelby!"

It didn't take us no more than fifteen minutes to the top of the hill again. We made good time taking ground but bayonets forced us to retreat again. I'm not sure whether we had to retreat two or three times. It didn't matter because the enemy lost men every time we moved on them. They lost more when they faced us with a bayonet charge. I don't reckon that they ever had a chance.

No! They didn't have a chance. We fired at them from the cover of the tree line while they fired in formation from the crest of the hill with no cover. When they made bayonet charges, they were forced out of formation by the brush and trees that offered us protection.

Our best shots, men like Josh Culbertson were put up high where they could fire at the British. They fired and most every time they fired, an enemy died.

Close to the enemy and behind trees, we did damage to our enemy. Some tried to mount a bayonet attack to push us back again but we had backed off enough. We counter attacked the line of bayonets with clubbed rifles, knives, tomahawks and by throwing rocks at them after our rifles were empty.

It was the beginning of the end. A man stood up and advanced with a white flag but was shot down. It is not known whether the man who fired the shot knew he was trying to surrender. Many of us had entered the battle afraid to surrender fearing we would receive 'Tarleton's quarter' rather than being allowed to surrender.

The thick gunpowder smoke made white flags harder to see

but many of our men did not want to give quarter. They had entered the battle expecting no quarter and did not trust any of Ferguson's men to surrender.

A British officer with about twenty-five mounted men tried to rally their forces and run us back down the mountain. They couldn't do it. I guess we were just too tired of coming up the hill to do it anymore. I saw a loyalist waving a white rag and moved to accept it when another Tory shot at me. The seventy-five caliber ball from his Brown Bess musket missed me but it sure fixed any ideas I had about accepting anybody's surrender.

The British circle kept shrinking and some Tory's were curled up, lying down. Some were praying.

I stopped shooting at any who were not holding a weapon.

Seeing that the battle was lost, Ferguson and a few of his men tried to ride down the south side of king's Mountain and escape by breaking through our line. He tried to ride through with sword in hand, slashing as he rode.

The word that Ferguson wore a light colored hunting frock over his clothing and used a sword in his left hand had been told to all of us. One of Sevier's men, a wounded man named Gilleland, saw Ferguson trying to get away. He tried to get Ferguson to stop but Ferguson paid him no attention. Gilleland tried to shoot him but his rifle misfired. He immediately called Rob Young.

"Rob, yonder goes Ferguson, shoot him!"

"I'll get him!"

Rob raised his rifle, which he called 'Sweet Lips,' aimed and fired. His shot hit Ferguson. Several others fired at Ferguson before he had fallen from his horse. Then Ferguson was down and all those trying to escape with him were killed or forced to retreat back to the British lines.

They rushed to Ferguson to find him either already dead or real close to it. I reckon they all knew he wouldn't be crossing the mountains with fire and sword like he had threatened to do.

We lost another of our officers late in the battle. Colonel Williams, who had been promoted after giving his account of the Battle of Musgrove's Mill to South Carolina's governor was killed. Reports were that he had died bravely.

The battle was ending. I was tired, thirsty and excited. I turned to find Nate beside me. I grinned at him and he grinned back.

"Dan, let's go find some shade and some water."

"You lead the way."

Epilogue

October 8, 1780

Dear Sally,

I hope this letter finds you well and that you were able to forgive me for leaving without saying goodbye. I knew that if I stopped to say goodbye that I would have had trouble leaving you and I did not wish to have your tears as the last memory of you.

I cherish the memory of the last time we were together and am constantly distracted by the memory of your kisses. After we are together, I will never leave you.

For now, we must be apart. The war and the danger of a British army coming over the mountains still remains. I feel that I now must continue to fight so that later you will be safe.

When the war is over, I will return. I pray that you will be waiting for me. Believe me, Sally, when I say that you are the only woman for me. I pray we will spend our lives together.

Now, Isaac Shelby and others have decided to remain and continue fighting the British. I will remain with them.

Yours

Daniel Bowman
December 5th, 1781

Sally read the letter again as she had read it every day since receiving it more than a year earlier. There had been no other letters and she had not been able to send one because she didn't know where to send it. She smoothed out the letter and placed it back in the Bible.

"Sally!"

"Yes Ma?"

"There's someone coming to see you. A man."

"If he's coming a sparkin, send him away."

"I sure believe he's coming a sparkin and I don't think we can run him off. Maybe you won't want to run him off."

Sally turned angrily. She had put the word out that she was spoken for and not interested in callers. The men still tried to come calling though.

"Sally!"

"Dan!"

Lifting her skirts so that she could run faster and without grabbing a shawl, Sally ran into the cool December evening and into Dan's arms.

She forgot all about scolding him for not stopping to say goodbye.

Author's Note

I can't help wondering if the Wataugans (overmountain people) would have paid any attention to Major Patrick Ferguson's threat to "come with fire and sword" if the British had not sent cannon and soldiers into Kentucky. Captain Byrd and his force with cannon were sent to Kentucky because the British in Detroit were afraid that George Rogers Clark would bring an army up and defeat them as he had defeated Henry (the hair buyer) Hamilton at Fort Sackville.

Without Byrd's demonstration into Kentucky, it is possible that Ferguson's threats would have been ignored due to the terrain and distance that separated him from their settlements.

Instead of ignoring Ferguson's threats, they elected to meet and defeat him. Defeating Ferguson on King's Mountain led to a shift in Cornwallis' tactics and strategy. This shift led to Tarleton being whipped like a borrowed mule at the Cowpens on January 17, 1781 by General Daniel Morgan.

This defeat led to Cornwallis destroying his wagons and any supplies that could not be carried and pursuing first Morgan and then General Nathaniel Green until Green and his army crossed the Dan River into Virginia - - - - - taking all boats to the Virginia side with him.

Cornwallis strutted back through North Carolina, claiming victory until he was aware that Green appeared to be chasing him. They met in battle at Guilford Court House on March 15, 1781. Cornwallis held the field but lost over one fourth of his men.

Without supplies and no new troops joining him, Cornwallis had three choices:
    1. Stay in North Carolina with insufficient provisions and

men.

2. Return to South Carolina where he would be subservient to Lord Rawdon.
3. Go north to Virginia where he would be the ranking officer and have access to supplies.

Cornwallis elected to move north into Virginia where he was forced to surrender his army at the Battle of Yorktown.

Was the fear of George Rogers Clark by the British in Detroit the first step to the British defeat at the Battle of Yorktown?

Possibly.

Other Books by Charles E. Hayes

Out of the Jungle

The Sword of Gideon

The life and Times of Ralph Marcum

Ambush at the Blue Licks

The Bloody Sevens

Boonesborough Attack

The Longhunter

Blood Debt

Kentucky Tales from the Old Man

Listening to Night Winds at Blue Licks

Kentucky Memories

Jimmy and Tommy Make Soap

About the Author

The author, Charles E. Hayes, MSgt, USAF (Ret.) spent 24 years in the United States Air Force. He is a former school teacher and an avid re- enactor. He currently helps other veterans through the auspices of the Disabled American Veterans in Kentucky. He lives in London Kentucky. He researches and writes full time.

Made in the USA
Charleston, SC
14 January 2016